The Visitor Paperback Copyright © 2023 Lorhainne Ekelund
Editor: Talia Leduc

ISBN-13: 978-1998775705

Give feedback on the book at:
lorhainneeckhart@hotmail.com

Twitter: @LEckhart
Facebook: AuthorLorhainneEckhart

Printed in the U.S.A

The Visitor

THE FRIESSENS
BOOK TWENTY-EIGHT

LORHAINNE ECKHART

"There are some people you can forgive and then there are those you can't!"

J. TULLOCH, REVIEWER

"When the past comes calling family love will prevail."

CATLOU, REVIEWER

"This book made my heart ache for Laura. I know how it feels to think one way about a person while everyone else thinks they are wonderful."

KEC200, REVIEWER

The Reunion
The Bloodline
The Promise
The Business Plan
The Decision
First Love
Family First
Leave the Light On
In the Moment
In the Family: A Friessen Family Christmas
In the Silence
In the Stars
In the Charm
Unexpected Consequences
It Was Always You
The First Time I Saw You
Welcome to My Arms
Welcome to Boston (A Paige & Morgan Short Story)
I'll Always Love You
Ground Rules
A Reason to Breathe
You Are My Everything
Anything For You
The Homecoming includes When They Were Young
Stay Away From My Daughter
The Bad Boy
A Place of Our Own
The Visitor
All About Devon
Long Past Dawn
How to Heal a Heart
Keep Me In Your Heart

The Friessen Family

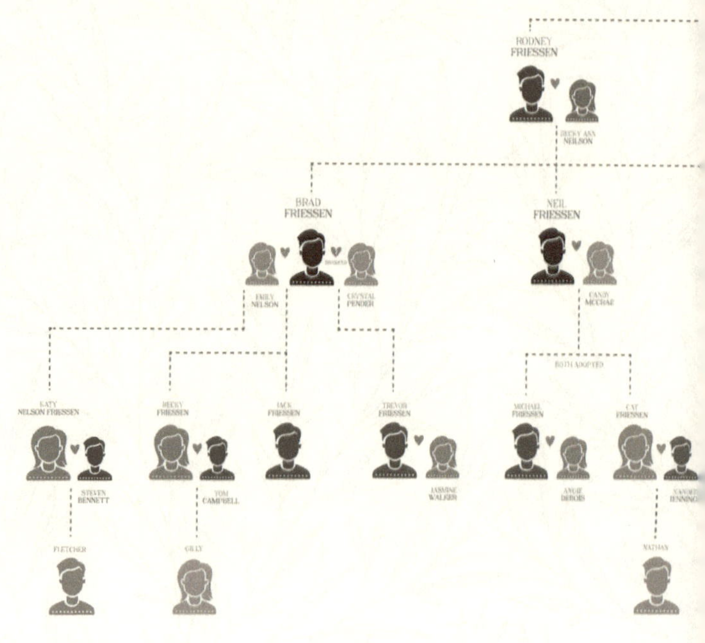

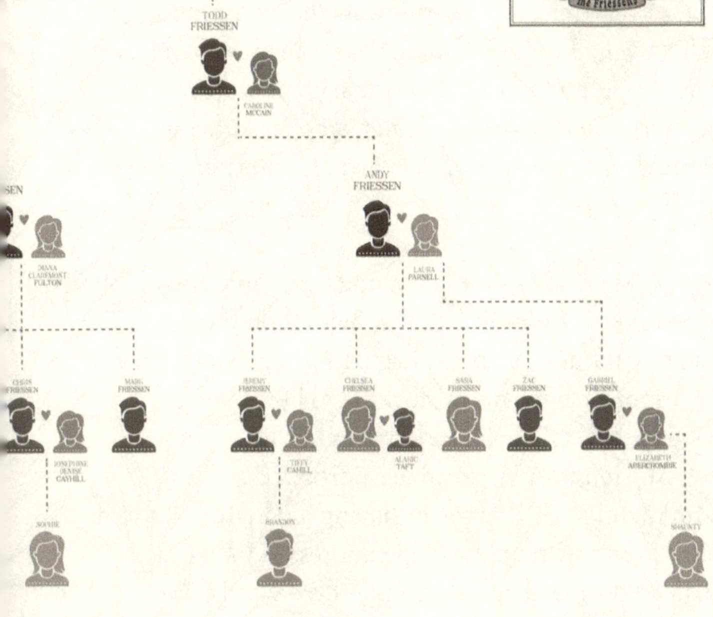

The Friessens

THE ENTIRE FRIESSEN FAMILY	
ANDY & LAURA	
JED & DIANA	
NEIL & CANDY	
BRAD & EMILY	
KATY & STEVEN	
KATY & STEVEN	

The Friessens

LEAVE THE LIGHT ON	KATY & STEVEN
IN THE MOMENT	BECKY & TOM
IN THE FAMILY *A Friessen Family Christmas*	THE ENTIRE FRIESSEN FAMILY
IN THE SILENCE	CAT & XANDER
IN THE STARS	DANNY & EVIE
IN THE CHARM	CHRIS & JD
UNEXPECTED CONSEQUENCES	CHRIS & JD

The Friessens

IT WAS ALWAYS YOU	KATY & STEVEN
THE FIRST TIME I SAW YOU	GABRIEL & ELIZABETH
WELCOME TO MY ARMS	CHELSEA & ALARIC
WELCOME TO BOSTON	PAIGE & MORGAN *A Friessen Spin-off*
I'LL ALWAYS LOVE YOU	JEREMY
GROUND RULES	JEREMY & TIFFY
A REASON TO BREATHE	TREVOR & JASMINE
YOU ARE MY EVERYTHING	MICHAEL & ANGIE
ANYTHING FOR YOU	*A Cat & Xander Brz Novella*
THE HOMECOMING	THE ENTIRE FRIESSEN FAMILY

New York Times & USA Today bestselling author Lorhainne Eckhart returns with a Friessen family character who must come to terms with unfinished business and long-buried hurts—not just for her family but for herself.

In Laura Friessen's peaceful, comfortable world, her family is everything, and at times she has to remind herself how lucky she is. These days, she gives barely a passing thought to her unsupportive, hypocritical parents or to her husband's father, who, as far as she's concerned, is a scourge on the earth. Good riddance to them all!

However, her world comes crashing down in a single day. First, her husband's father shows up on their doorstep without a penny to his name, believing Laura is solely responsible for his misfortune in life. Then an article appears online about her parents, who run a church mission in Africa and are portrayed as saints, with no mention of them ever having a daughter. Last, a courier arrives with an envelope addressed to her, with no return address, containing only three words: _You owe me!_

Laura believes this is Andy's father's pathetic attempt at revenge, at extracting what he believes he's entitled to. She knows that if they let Todd Friessen through the door, he'll attempt to manipulate not only Andy but also their children and grandchildren, who don't know the man who now wants to be called Grandfather.

Unfortunately, what Laura doesn't realize is that even though she has an amazing life, before she can move forward into her future, she has to confront her past.

CHAPTER
One

The horses had been herded into the corral, and Laura could hear them nicker as she watched Jeremy and Tiffy come out of the barn, where they lived in the loft, which had been transformed into their apartment. There was something comforting about having her family close, something that had her breathing a little easier.

Tiffy was dressed in capris and a floral tee, her hair pulled high in a ponytail, evidently on her way to work. Laura's three-year-old grandson, Brandon, was between them, jumping, running, reminding her so much of Jeremy at that age. Being called Grandma warmed her heart even though she wasn't yet forty.

She took in her son with his gorgeous young wife. Jeremy was tall and handsome just like his father, dressed in blue jeans and a faded blue shirt. As she watched the kiss between the two, she was reminded of how much he still needed to learn about life, about marriage. Tiffy climbed into her small Subaru wagon, leaving Jeremy holding Brandon's hand. They waved to her as she pulled away.

Laura lingered at the kitchen window, rinsing the last of the breakfast dishes from the fruit and granola she and Andy had shared. Zac had left a pile of toast crumbs before going back to bed, and she suspected Sara was still sleeping until she heard a creak from somewhere in the house. Obviously, Sara was up, and maybe Zac too, considering it was Saturday and Andy had insisted they help with the cattle.

She heard footsteps, voices, Andy and Jeremy laughing before they opened the door with a creak. She couldn't have explained to anyone why having her family close gave her a sense of peace, one she had to remind herself every day that she was entitled to and deserved. It was the kind of life she never could have imagined for herself.

"Told you I need both you and Zac to help move the herd today," Andy said to Jeremy as they strode into the kitchen. "Time to bring them into the north field. It's an all-day job."

His boots scraped the floor, just clean from the day before, and he reached for a mug in the cupboard. Why did no one seem to realize the time it took to keep this place clean?

Laura pulled at the tie of the silky green robe around her waist, her bare feet on the hardwood floor. She knew she should hop in the shower, but there was something she appreciated about lingering in the morning with another coffee and having a minute or two to herself.

"Grandma, I'm hungry. Can I have a cookie?" Brandon said. He had Jeremy's dark wavy hair, and his eyes held that same smart mischievousness her son had been known for, always thinking he was pulling one over on them.

"You just ate breakfast, Brandon. No cookies..." Jeremy started, but Laura reached into the Cookie Monster jar and held out a peanut butter cookie to Brandon.

"Just one," she said. Her grandson gave her a big smile, and she took in Jeremy's frown and Andy shaking his head as she offered them both one of the batch she'd made just the day before.

"Mom, you're not helping," Jeremy said, though he grabbed three from the jar and shoved one in his mouth as he talked. Andy took a bite, made a sound of appreciation, and then leaned in and kissed her.

"He had breakfast, and it's just one. You were worse," Laura said. She settled the lid back on the cookie jar after taking one herself.

Jeremy made a rude noise. She knew he didn't remember how he and his twin sister, Chelsea, had never given her a moment's rest. From his first step, he had taken off at a run, getting into anything and everything. He turned back to Andy, who was staring down at Brandon.

"I have to work this afternoon at two, so we'd need to saddle the horses and start now," Jeremy said. "I'll have to cut out early if we don't finish. I was going to take Brandon to Tiffy's parents' place to hang out for the day."

Andy was shaking his head. "If everyone pitches in, we should be done before then. Brandon can stay here with your mom."

She listened to what she knew was the bathroom

door closing, likely Sara, as Zac wandered in. He was almost as tall as his dad and brother, but he had that lanky teenage build, his eyes glued to his cell phone, texting something as he walked. His hair was a mess as he reached for the loaf of bread and popped a few slices into the toaster, then pulled open the cupboard and reached for a box of cornflakes. He was a bottomless pit and could've eaten them out of house and home.

"Grandpa, I want to come to ride my horsey. I help too." Brandon was jumping.

Andy lifted him up and kissed his cheek. "Nope, not this time. You're too young, and it's too dangerous. Grandpa will take you out on your pony tomorrow, but today you can stay here with Grandma. Zac, you need to shake a leg. We're going to be moving the herd, and I need you out there."

Zac had poured cereal into one of their large serving bowls and dumped milk over it, and he was shoving it in his mouth. "Fine," he mumbled around a mouthful, milk dripping down his faded brown T-shirt.

Andy slid his gaze over to her. She wondered whether he had any idea how much she loved him, whether he knew that she felt as if this life she'd settled into with her family was just a dream that could be yanked away. "Sara up? I need her out there, too," Andy said. He had poured more coffee and leaned against the counter to take a swallow.

"Likely just up, but Sara can look after Brandon while I have a shower and get dressed," Laura said. She wasn't sure what to make of Andy's smile, but she knew he enjoyed the mornings they shared a shower. She did, too, even though it didn't happen as often as she liked.

"Hey, Mom, aren't these your parents?" Sara said as

she walked into the kitchen, her long blond hair a tousled mess, wearing a white tank and sweatpants. She was holding her cell phone.

What was it about her kids and their never-ending need for their devices, their social media accounts, and texting everyone? She wondered at times if they saw anything that went on in the outside world. She didn't move as Sara held up the Android screen, showing an article with a photo of her parents, whom she hadn't seen in some twenty years. It was a punch to her gut, and for a second, she forgot to breathe.

"George and Sue Parnell, voted parents of the year by the Midwest Baptists. Their two grown sons are following in their father's footsteps in the church, with their missionary work in Africa, and the people they've helped…"

Sara was reading the article aloud, but Laura just stared in horror at the smiling image of her parents, who were so much older now, and her brothers, whom she'd also lost touch with. They were the perfect image of the perfect family who loved and adored each other, and even to her, they looked like the kind of family people would see as role models.

As she scanned the article, which talked about how wonderful they were, all the sacrifices they'd made, and the fine sons they'd raised, their morals, their values, their principles, she realized there was no mention of her—just them and the perfect image of the family they were.

"Uh, yeah…" Her throat thickened, and she could feel Andy looking down, reading. He was pressed against her, so close.

"What is that?" Zac asked, or maybe it was Jeremy. She was only half listening as she stared at the article.

It had to be a mistake. She scanned it again, looking for some hint, some mention of a daughter, but there was nothing. It was as if she'd never existed to them, and she couldn't explain to anyone how raw the ache still was. Weren't all children supposed to be loved and supported by their parents?

Andy powered off the screen and pulled the phone away, handing it back to Sara. Of course, he knew. It was an ache that just didn't go away. Andy had said to her time and again that they didn't matter. She knew to them she was a disappointment, and her parents would never accept her, all because she'd gotten pregnant at fifteen. She pulled in another breath.

"You know what? It's not worth reading," Andy said. "They're not family, and let's just leave it at that. Sara, why don't you give us a hand moving the cattle?"

Sara had that look on her face, one Laura knew well. She was curious and wanted the scoop, wanted to know all the dirt on her folks. Laura had never shared anything with her kids other than to confirm that yes, she had parents and brothers, but they were estranged. End of story.

"Not this time. Sorry, Dad," Sara said. "I have to get ready to go out. I'm meeting Devon and have that appointment with school." She lifted Brandon, who was always hanging off her. She was good with him—no, great.

Laura had to turn away, as the memory of that smiling image of her parents was like a knife stabbing her in the heart. Then the article, parents of the year… seriously? She wasn't sure what Andy said to Sara, as she was only half listening, staring through the window above the sink.

Then Andy was right beside her, and she didn't have to look over to know how he was watching her. There was his touch, his hand sliding over hers. He didn't have to say a word. It was there. He did, though, lean down and kiss her cheek.

"Forget them. It means nothing," he said.

She knew what he was saying, but at the same time, it hurt more than she knew was reasonable, that feeling of being unwanted. She and Andy had created the kind of family she'd never had, a family that was her everything. She nodded as her throat thickened. His touch said everything, and she could hear her kids talking in the background as Andy leaned in and kissed her again, as if it was just her and him.

"Go shower," he said. "Sara will watch Brandon." His voice was low, and his gaze lingered a second as his hand grazed her cheek. Then he stepped away, her hand sliding over his arm. "After your mom showers, Sara, you meet us out in the south field. Your life is on hold until the cattle are moved. Devon can wait, but the cattle won't."

She took in the stubborn yet angelic look her daughter always pulled with Andy before she rolled her eyes. "Fine, but not all day, Dad…"

Andy lifted his hand as Jeremy and Zac stepped out of the kitchen. "Yeah, I know, you have a life that's not centered on this ranch or these cattle, and that's far more exciting than following a bunch of noisy cows. You've made that clear. At the same time, this pays the bills and provides for this family, which you're still a part of. Are we clear?" he said. She waited for Sara to add something, but Andy shook his head and made a face as he glanced at her. "Don't be long."

As he stepped out of the kitchen, she listened to the squeak of the screen door. Everything about her family was so chaotic, always butting heads, but they were perfect. Still, she couldn't get the image of the family she'd grown up in out of her head. They were so alien to her, yet the image had brought with it a dreadful ache in her gut, as if someone had reached in and squeezed. It was a past she'd thought she'd closed the door on.

"So it's just us now, and…" Sara said, putting Brandon down and glancing at him. He was standing there, watching her and Sara. Smart kid. "Hey, bud, go play, scram," Sara said, and Laura watched as Brandon took off to the family room and pulled out his box of cars. "So, Mom, why is there an article about your parents, your brothers, and no mention of you?"

There it was. How could she explain to her daughter that not everyone had the kind of family that would stand by them through thick and thin?

"It's just the way they are, Sara. I'm their disappointment."

Her daughter's eyes widened.

"It bothered me once and still does, even though it shouldn't—but at the same time, you know what?" she said.

Her daughter didn't pull her gaze from her. She said nothing as she waited, then shrugged.

"I have you guys and your dad," Laura said. "We're close and love each other, even though there are times I want to pull my hair out at some of the choices you make and the things you do. We're all I need, so they don't matter. They're from another lifetime. As a kid, you can't pick your family, but you can when you're an adult. What happened to me is not the kind of thing a parent should be proud of. No, your dad is right, and he's said this to me time and again. They're the ones who should be ashamed, and maybe they are, since it's evidently easier for them to pretend I don't exist, to never mention me, than to explain how that image of a model family they're putting out to the world is false. They're hypocrites, but they'd never want to be labeled as such. Perfection is what they want—and to control how they're seen by everyone." She wondered how she hadn't thought of that before, and she took in the smile that touched her daughter's lips.

"You're right, Mom. Though I have to say, I sometimes wondered what they were like and was curious to meet them and know them."

Maybe the shock on her face was what had her daughter reaching over and rubbing her arm with a teasing smile.

"Relax, Mom. I said 'wondered.' We all have, but you know what? We're awesome, and we really don't need anyone like that in our lives, hypocrites who pretend to be something they're not. I mean, look at us. Just how would they react if they met us?"

She stared at her daughter. When had she become so wise? At the same time, she did wonder what her parents would think of her kids. "Good point. Sara, they don't deserve to know you."

Sara winked. "You got it, Mom. So you have about twenty minutes to shower and get dressed, and then I need to get ready, because Dad is on the warpath, insisting I help move the herd even though he knows I need to get ready and have stuff to do."

She took in her daughter, who was in an on-again, off-again relationship with Devon. "What stuff?"

Her daughter shrugged, smiled, and stretched. "Well, Devon's coming over, or rather, he's picking me up, and we're heading into town today. I have a life too, Mom." Then Sara's phone dinged, and she pulled her gaze away, smiled, and answered.

Laura didn't have to ask who it was. She knew it was Devon, the tall, dark, and handsome boyfriend who had saved her. That teenage love, which Laura knew well, was quickly turning into something serious.

She turned to look out the window again when she saw a minivan she didn't recognize driving up the dirt road to the house. She was still wearing her housecoat, yet the way today was going, it seemed as if her peaceful, quiet morning was turning into anything but.

"Mom, it's addressed to you, and the guy at the door says you need to sign for it!" Sara called out.

Laura had only just managed to run a brush through her hair after pulling on trackpants and a T-shirt—forget the shower—when she pulled open the door of the master bedroom and hurried down the hall, barefoot.

The man at the door had brown hair and was average height, maybe thirtyish. She didn't know why she felt as if someone had taken hold of her stomach and squeezed. Sara appeared amused as she waited with Brandon beside her, staring at the strange man who was standing just outside, propping open the screen door with his foot.

"Fine, fine. What is it, anyways?" she called. What was it that felt so off about the man and the way he held his clipboard? Sure, he was somewhat tall, but he had nothing on her husband. For a minute, she had to rack her brain, trying to remember whether Andy had said to expect a delivery.

"Are you Laura Friessen?" The man's twang was local, and the lisp was irritating.

"Mm-hmm, that's me. Again, what is this?" She flicked her gaze to the clipboard, the envelope, and the type on the letter, just her name and address.

"A delivery. Need you to sign for it." He slid the clipboard around to reveal a list of names and signatures on a page that was both dirty and dog-eared, likely from all the other deliveries. She scribbled her name and took the letter, wondering why it was so important that she'd had to sign for it.

"So who's it from? It doesn't say." She flipped it over.

The man stepped onto the front porch, his hand still on the screen door, and shrugged. "No idea. I just deliver. You all have a nice day, you hear?" His boots were ratty, his blue shirt faded, and he strode back to a minivan that had seen better days.

"Well? Open it," Sara said, that curious light in her eyes, so Laura slid her finger under the crease and ripped it open, then pulled out a single sheet that was folded over.

"Likely some marketing scheme," she said. "You know, they get a hold of your name and go to all these extraordinary lengths just so you'll buy whatever they're…" She flicked open the paper and stared at the big bold print, just three words: *YOU OWE ME!* For a second, she forgot to breathe. Okay, this was absolutely crazy.

"Uh, Mom, is this some kind of joke?" she vaguely heard Sara say. She just stared at the paper, looking for anything else, but it was just those three words. She flipped it over a second time, because she had to be missing something. Was it a joke? Maybe, considering her morning thus far. Even the envelope didn't leave a clue.

She glanced over to her daughter, who was so much taller than she was, gorgeous and leggy. Thankfully, she had her head screwed on right, but that did nothing to help with this bizarre letter. Why was it addressed to her? She stared at the envelope again. Yup, just her name, their address.

She lifted her hands, then folded the letter and tucked it back into the envelope, confused and irritated that someone would think sending her this as a joke was in any way funny.

"Let me see it." Sara took the envelope, and Laura stared at the trail of dust from the minivan as it drove away. Hadn't he said he had no idea who it was from? That was a lot of trouble, hiring a courier to send something that made no sense.

"Maybe it's a joke, or they addressed it to the wrong person," Laura said. Or maybe she owed someone something—but who would that be? She'd never taken anything from anyone in her life.

"Or maybe it's some mysterious person who's trying to blackmail you or Dad or both of you. Maybe a former boyfriend, Mom, or someone who thinks you've done something to them, or…"

Laura took in Brandon and the way he was watching, listening, and frowning, and she reached over and ripped the envelope from her daughter's hand. "Or maybe it's a big mistake and it was addressed to the wrong person. It happens." She walked back into the kitchen and slipped it with the other mail and bills and junk she hadn't tossed away yet by the back door. Time for her to go through it all and clean it out.

"Mom, you're no fun, seriously. But that's just plain weird… What kind of sicko would send that in a letter? I bet it's Chels or Ric trying to mess with you," Sara said, then shrugged, likely at the way Laura was staring at her. "Okay, so I'm reaching."

"Mm-hmm," Laura said. "Although Chels likes to tease, she wouldn't do that, and Ric? I think not."

The unsettling letter had her thinking of everyone she'd ever had problems with. Yeah, there were a few, such as her son Gabriel's father, Brian, who'd signed away his rights. Then there were the staff from when she'd worked as a maid in Andy's parents' mansion, just a young girl with a son, down on her luck. It seemed as if that was a different Laura from a different time, but some of the staff likely couldn't believe she was still married to Andy. Then there was Andy's mother. Though she was now dead, her family was still out there. There was also her own family, all those people who'd treated her as if she was no one as she struggled alone with Gabriel. And lastly, there was Andy's father, Todd. She pressed her hands to her eyes and rubbed. She was going to drive herself crazy, thinking about this.

"Hey, Mom, you don't think this has anything to do with what went down in Cancun, do you?" Sara said.

Laura pressed her hand to the counter, feeling gritty and still wanting a shower. Her too-smart, impression-able grandson was still listening to everything. Maybe she should consider a bath, give herself time to sort out all of this craziness. Her day was heading in a direction that wasn't all that comforting.

"Does a bad man want to hurt you, Grandma?"

Laura leaned down to Brandon, taking in his innocent green eyes, the same as hers and all her kids, even though she could see so much of Andy, of Tiffy, of everyone in him. "Don't you worry," she said. "It's nothing, just someone messing with me, a joke. So listen, why don't you go pop on the TV and watch some cartoons?"

He frowned, and the way he furrowed his brow was so cute. "But you know Mom doesn't let me watch TV during the day…" he replied. Had he seriously said that?

"And you know what? Your mom's not here. This is Grandma's time, and I say you can go watch some cartoons. I'm going to shower, and your auntie is going to look after you, and then you can go out and join your dad and grandpa and uncle Zac in herding up the cows. Then you can help Grandma…"

Help her do what? He was a little boy who wanted to run and play and spend time outside with Andy, Jeremy, and the horses—but not today. She knew Andy didn't want him anywhere near the herd while he was moving the cattle, or while the hay was delivered, or while he was deworming, or while he was doing anything that could lead to Brandon being hurt in any way. She knew Andy needed to keep his focus, and she realized he was also trying to respect Tiffy's fear of horses. That was just another thing she loved about him.

Sara rested her hand on Brandon's head. "Yeah, bud, it'll be you and me for a bit. I'll make breakfast, and then…"

There was another knock at the door, and she wasn't sure who was more shocked, her or Sara.

"I didn't hear a car," she said. Of course, her first thought was the courier. Maybe he'd figured out the mistake and had come back to tell her, or maybe he was in on the joke.

Brandon was already running to the door, and Sara followed him. Laura pulled in a shaky breath, convinced now that a bath definitely topped a shower. She ran her hands over her face and swept back her hair as she heard voices: Sara and a man.

His voice was deep and familiar, bringing a sick feeling to the pit of her stomach and making her dig into each step a little more as an icy chill settled in her bones. She had to be wrong.

As she rounded the corner, her toe stubbed on one of Brandon's toy cars, and she swore and hopped. When she looked up, she saw the graying hair, icy blue eyes, and distinguished features of Todd Friessen. It was impossible, yet there he was, neatly shaven, his hair short. His clothes were tasteful, blue jeans and a maroon dress shirt under a leather jacket—clean, neat, new. He wore a gold ring on his finger, and the chain around his neck settled in his thick chest hair, which was visible from the open top button of his shirt.

"Laura," he said.

Laura glanced to Sara, who stared at her and Todd. Brandon also seemed confused. She breathed from her open mouth and just stared, no words coming to her.

"Mom, who is this?" Sara asked.

Todd stepped inside, and the door squeaked shut. She didn't move, forcing herself to swallow. How was it that she could still feel so small around a man who didn't hold any power over her? She felt herself tossed back to a time when he had.

Todd pulled his shrewd gaze from her and gave everything to her daughter, and the look had Laura's fear and rage simmering. Then he was staring down at Brandon, so she moved closer and stood in front of him so Todd Friessen couldn't see him, touch him, talk to him.

Her hand was on his shoulder just as Todd said, "I'm your grandfather. So where is my son?" He flicked his gaze over to her, and she reached for Brandon's hand, holding it and stepping back, smelling Todd's cologne and the way he allowed his gaze to settle again on Sara and soften.

"Why are you here?" was all she could say, fighting the urge to tell Sara to go to her room, to call her father so he could tell Todd to get out of her house.

"Is that any way to greet me?" he replied. It sounded as if he felt entitled, but then, that was all he'd ever been. He shook his head. "I came a long way. Aren't you going to invite me in? After all, we're family, I came to meet my grandkids, to see my son. This is about family, my family."

There it was, the way he looked at her again with that same predatory icy gaze—and something else. The way he watched her, she figured he wasn't there to make amends. No, Todd was staring at her with such hate that it was no wonder she felt as if she was going to puke. Wow, how much worse could this day get?

"I think you're confused," she replied. "This is my family, not yours. You may be Andy's father, but that's all you are." She turned to Sara, not missing the shock on her face. She opened her mouth to say something, but Laura touched her arm and said, "Call your dad. Tell him—"

"Tell my son that his father is here," Todd said, never pulling his hard gaze from her. The way he stared her down, he was expecting her to retreat. To hell with him! "And then…Sara, is it? I think it's time I got to know all my grandkids. After all, blood is everything. You're my blood, and once upon a time, your dad and I were close. And you know what? That kind of closeness never really goes away."

The way he said the last bit, Laura realized he was trying to rattle her, and it was working. She turned to Sara and gestured with her chin. "Call your dad, and take Brandon with you."

Sara stared at her, a clear question in her eyes, before murmuring something to Brandon and slipping with him back into the kitchen.

Laura gave everything to a man she despised and feared, worried he could still have the kind of hold on her husband that he once had. She knew that couldn't be possible, though.

"You're still mighty fetching there, Laura," Todd said. The smile that touched his handsome features had her wrapping her arms over her chest, feeling so exposed.

"So why are you really here, Todd?" she replied. It was the first time she'd ever said his first name, having always called him Mr. Friessen. It felt odd. She felt out of place in her own home.

"I told you: to see my son, to meet my grandkids— and to settle something that's been a long time coming."

The way he said it only deepened the icy chill that had settled in her stomach moments earlier. How could all of this, her peaceful, comfortable life, suddenly be wiped away?

CHAPTER

Three

All she wanted was a bath to soak away what was turning into a really shitty morning, the worst of the worst. She couldn't fight the worry at what else could possibly be coming her way. It was the kind of feeling she hadn't experienced in years. It was humbling, and she missed her peaceful, quiet existence. She couldn't shake the feeling that this strange start to the day had shaken up her happy life with her family, and nothing would ever be the same again. Why now? Why her? What had she done?

She held the phone to her ear as she stood just inside the kitchen, her hand resting on the island, taking in the breadcrumbs and spilled milk from Zac's rushed breakfast. Andy's phone rang a second time before it went to voicemail again: "This is Andy. You can leave a message, or if you need to get a hold of me, send an email."

Everyone hated his message, but he insisted on using it because everyone thought they could call any time and expect him to drop everything at a moment's notice. She wasn't about to email him, though, because she'd see him long before he thought to check all his emails.

"Andy, please call me at home. Your dad's here. He's in the house. He's talking to Sara, to Brandon, and…"

She'd never even invited him in. The man had walked in and taken over, still ordering her around, and what had she done? Nothing. She'd shrunk back into that young woman without a voice. She'd seen the way he still looked at her as if she was his servant. Damn him! She hated feeling this way and needed to remind herself she had a voice, and this was her home.

She disconnected the phone and squeezed the handset. She could hear him still talking to Sara, giving that same laugh, as if he were someone of importance. Through the kitchen window, she spotted Andy's two trucks, her SUV, Jeremy's truck, and a silver BMW. So that was what Todd had driven. She'd never heard him pull in.

"Shit," she said, tapping her fingers on the counter. What was she going to do? She should go dig out her cell phone, which was likely dead because she never used it. Texting Zac or Jeremy would be a sure-fire way to reach one of them and get Andy to ride in and take care of his father. Zac never parted with his phone, and Jeremy was just as likely to respond right away.

She spotted her purse hanging at the back door and rummaged inside before pulling out her cell phone. Todd was still talking with her daughter, and she fought her panic at the idea of Sara or Brandon being anywhere near him. She pressed the button to power on her iPhone, seeing the screen light up, and for a second the relief was indescribable. She couldn't believe it worked.

She pulled in a breath, knowing she should feel relieved, but her hand was shaking. She glanced up and pulled in another breath, and this time she sent Andy a text.

Your dad's here. I already left you a voicemail!!!

Nothing. No dots to show he'd read it and was replying, but then, he didn't live with his cell phone in hand as though it held all the answers in the world. She texted Zac next.

Are you with your dad? Tell him to check his damn phone and call me now! His father showed up here. Tell him to come home now.

She waited for the familiar three dots to show, but there was nothing. She texted Jeremy next.

911! I need your dad now! Are you there?

Nothing. Shit! Of all times for her kids to put aside their phones. "Dammit," she breathed out, staring at the lack of replies.

She dumped her cell phone on the counter and forced herself to turn around and go into the living room to face Todd, at the same time wishing Andy were there to do something and tell his father to go away, leave them be, and never bother them again.

Her feet were bare, and she felt naked and exposed under her T-shirt and sweats. She needed a bra and some underwear, to at least splash water on her face and brush her teeth, but that would mean leaving Todd alone with Sara and Brandon, whom she loved more than her next breath. She couldn't do that—she wouldn't. She was freaking out over the fact that they were with him now.

She stared at the landline again, willing it to ring, then took in the living room, where Todd was sitting in the easy chair as if holding court. Maybe he expected something from her, a coffee, a drink, a sandwich. Sara was on the sofa, Brandon beside her, sitting so quiet and good, and Todd was giving everything to them. He watched them as if they were everything and she didn't even exist, as if he were the one in charge in her house. How could anyone walk in and do this? Evidently, Todd Friessen could. The man still made her skin crawl and made her feel as if she was nothing.

"Andy will be here soon," she said as she took another step into the living room. "Sara, why don't you take Brandon outside? You were going to help with the herd. You know where your dad is." She hoped Sara knew what she meant and could see the panic she was doing her best to hide.

Sara seemed confused, and she noted the look, the hesitation, or was she about to argue? But she said nothing, then nodded as she glanced down to Brandon, having picked up on what was becoming a full-blown panic attack.

"Nonsense," Todd said. "I came all this way to see my grandkids. I have a right to know them and for them to know me. They can stay. I'll see my son when he gets here."

Her hands were crossed over her chest, and she squeezed under her arms, feeling the dampness of her cotton T-shirt. Of course, she was sweating. "Sara, I believe I said something to you." She let her full gaze land on Sara, who stood, realizing Laura meant business, even though she took in Todd again. Laura wondered for a second whether her daughter would go along with him.

"Uh, sure, Mom. Come on, Brandon." Sara took

Brandon's hand, and, thankfully, he went with her. She stopped beside Laura, a worried question in her eyes. "You okay, Mom?" Her voice was low, soft, just above a whisper.

Laura wondered whether Todd could hear. She hoped not and cleared her throat roughly. "Just go. I'm fine."

"But Dad said no to Brandon being around the cattle. What do you want me to do?"

Laura had to pull in another breath. Right. Andy wouldn't be happy. Panic and fear coursed through her. She was making a mess of things. She blinked, feeling again as though she couldn't breathe. She wondered why it had started today.

"Leave Brandon," she said. "Go, saddle up, and tell him to hurry. He's not answering his cell, and Zac and Jeremy aren't responding to my texts…"

It was in that moment that Sara seemed to get it. Considering there was so much she and Andy hadn't shared with the kids about his father, his family, she knew Sara had to have at least a dozen questions, if not more.

She watched as Sara let go of Brandon and shoved her bare feet into boots, then pulled a gray hoodie out of the front closet and shrugged it on before zipping it up. She stepped out, took a look back, and Brandon ran to the door.

"I want to go!" he called out.

"No, Brandon, stay here," Sara said. "Your grandpa said he didn't want you out with him today. You stay with Grandma."

Laura listened as Sara went down the steps, then hurried to the barn. She knew Todd Friessen hadn't pulled his gaze from her, watching her with disgust and dislike. He hadn't tried to hide it.

Her back ached. He had to see how rattled she was, but at the same time, she couldn't afford to let him know all her hard-earned confidence had disappeared in one moment of being alone with him. She forced herself not to cower under him or look his way as she rested her hands on Brandon's shoulders.

"Hey, come with Grandma. I'll give you two cookies, and you can watch cartoons. Can you do that for Grandma?" She somehow had him racing into the kitchen, and she followed. As she handed him two cookies from the jar, she knew she was doing the one thing she and Tiffy had been hounding Jeremy to stop doing.

She took a second as she watched him flick on the TV and settle down on the small taupe sectional. Okay, another of her flock was out of the way. She knew her time was up. She couldn't stall. She needed to go face the man who'd tried to end everything she had with her husband. She took a step and then another, seeing him standing in the living room, taking in the family photos on the wall—from Chelsea's wedding, from when the kids were small, from over the years, all of them together, all those special moments that connected them and her and Andy's love for each other. He had to see it. His back was to her. She could hear him breathing.

"So you've made something of yourself."

She wasn't sure whether she jumped. He hadn't turned around as he continued to take in all the images of her children, Gabriel and Elizabeth and Shaunty, Chelsea and Ric, Jeremy and Tiffy and Brandon, Sara and Zac. The moments that showed their love.

Then he turned around, and she could see some of his resemblance to her husband. "And my son gave up everything. Wonder if he still sees the choice he made as the right one."

For a second, she didn't know what to say. How could he say something so cruel, making her think she could in any way be responsible for her husband having given up everything for her?

"All my grandchildren?" he said, gesturing to the wall behind him. "They've grown."

She said nothing, just crossed her arms.

"Well, at least you were good for something," he said.

For another second, she forgot to breathe, but then she heard the flutter of her lungs working again. She wondered whether Todd knew what he was doing to her. "If you came here to insult me…"

He started laughing. It was deep and had her wanting to back up, but she couldn't do that. She wouldn't cower. She wouldn't let him do that to her in her house. "Insult you? No, not something I've ever been accused of. Brash, disgusting, rude, confident, direct, chauvinistic, a pig. I believe my son still made the biggest mistake of his life, taking up with you, putting a ring on your finger. He could have done so much better. He had his fun, I told him. All because of you, I lost everything I worked for, everything I earned and spent my life waiting to have, everything my son should have had. I mean, who are you, really? You're nothing, just a mistake—though, I admit, a pretty one. Yet here you are, still married to my son. At least you provided him children. At least you could do that much. I had everything, and I still can't believe he chose you over his blood, over me."

Had he ever been so cruel? It ached even though she knew it wasn't true. It couldn't be. "You're blaming me for what, exactly?" Was that her voice? She'd stood her ground and didn't move even though he took another step closer to her. Would he touch her, reach out to her, treat her like every woman he saw as just a plaything for him?

He laughed again, but now she heard voices outside. Andy.

Thank God! The relief was indescribable. His feet pounded the stairs, and the door flew open. His eyes were icy blue, his expression dark. It was something she hadn't seen in a long time. He seemed to take in everything—Todd, her. He let his gaze linger on her as he walked her way.

"You okay?" he said.

She nodded, but her breath caught. He walked past her, in front of her, and she lifted her hand to touch him but reached only air, as he kept moving toward his father.

"What are you doing here?" Andy's voice was accusing.

She heard voices outside, Jeremy, Zac, Sara, all of them on the stairs. The door squeaked, and they stepped inside, their expressions a mix of surprise and shock. She could almost hear the questions they now had to have.

"I came to see you, my boy," Todd said. "Hey, hey, are these my grandsons?" His face seemed to light up as Jeremy and Zac strode in. Sara stopped beside her, and she watched in horror as her sons stepped in past their dad and went over to a man she figured was only one step above a snake. She didn't hear what they said, but Jeremy held out his hand. "None of that," Todd replied. "I'm your grandfather. Come here, you two." He hugged both her kids, laughed, and she felt Sara's hand on her arm.

"Mom, are you okay?" Sara said. She looked worried, and what the hell was Laura supposed to say? They'd opened the door to someone despicable. Todd Friessen had fathered Andy, but he was the family she hadn't chosen.

CHAPTER

Four

Laura lifted her hand in the water and listened to the silence of her bathroom as she lingered in the soaker tub, feeling safer and cocooned. The sounds of the house, the voices that drifted in, sounded much like a hum in the distance.

She knew Todd Friessen was still there with her husband, her kids, and she knew the questions they had to have. That was the reason she was now alone in the bath in their bedroom, trying to make sense of this insanity, of what had been the start to a really shitty day. For a second, she had to fight the worry at what else could possibly show up to smack her upside the head and take her down once and for all.

She shut her eyes and leaned back, running her wet hands over her face and pulling her hair up in a messy bun. She wasn't sure what had her looking up, but there was Andy, leaning in the doorway, watching her. His expression seemed tired, and his emotions, she could already tell, seemed so mixed.

She wondered what he was thinking, feeling. He

made a face, and she took in the lines etched around his eyes, the gray now mixing with his dark hair, which made him even more handsome than when she'd first seen him years earlier as a young, stupid girl. He was still so tall, so broad-shouldered, the love of her life.

He leaned against the door frame and then lifted his hand and rubbed his face, his faded blue shirtsleeves rolled up to reveal dirt on his forearms. Just looking at him, she could see the resemblance to his father. It was around his eyes, in his expression. Why hadn't she noticed before?

"You didn't ask him to leave," she said. She pressed her hand to her chest, feeling the way her heart beat, the way her chest ached. She had to remind herself to breathe.

Andy sat on the edge of the tub and let his hand drop in the water as it skimmed over hers, her arm, her breast. She loved the feel of his touch, the roughness of his skin, his large hands. He pulled it away and rested it on his leg, and she could see the confliction as he said, "I never expected to see him, not after everything that happened. What did he say to you?"

She made a face and moved to sit up, pulling her knees against her chest. It wasn't even lunchtime yet and the day had already gone to shit. She rested her hand on his blue-jeaned leg and wondered how to explain how much Todd Friessen despised her. Even the words he'd said to her, she didn't know how to speak them so that Andy understood. Todd had never come right out and said anything horrible. Instead, the words had been there in the way he looked down on her, at her, through her. It had been so loud and clear as he danced around it and said everything but.

Andy would think she was crazy. Todd Friessen had never said how much he hated her, but it had been there in his eyes. He blamed her for him having nothing, for all his misfortune.

"What do you want me to say, Andy? He despises me, always has. Why is he here?"

He just stared at her. She could always tell when he was thinking of what to say. "He says he wants to meet his grandkids, get to know them, see me and try to repair our relationship. We were close when I was young, and I suspect he wants that back. I don't know. He's older now, not a young man. Maybe he has regrets? Another chance, some kind of relationship." He shrugged.

What was that? Andy never shrugged. She wondered if he really believed that or if it was something he wanted to believe. Like, where had that come from? Andy had made it clear his father was out of his life. After all, he was the scourge of the earth, all about money, position, power. That was the way of the world. She believed love, to him, was meaningless—except, maybe, his love for his son.

She wondered whether she made a face, as she could feel how on edge Andy was. "You seriously don't believe that, do you?" she said. "This is your father we're talking about, who has only ever been all about himself. Coming in here and looking down on me as if I'm no one, as if the only thing I've done right has been to give you more kids…" She could hear how bitter she sounded.

Andy's gaze was hard. He pulled in a breath and glanced away, around the bathroom, and back to her. "You know my father has never respected women."

It took her a second to understand what he was saying. It sounded like an excuse. "I know that, Andy, but at the same time, he doesn't get a pass for treating me and all women like crap."

He furrowed his brow, and she knew he wasn't understanding, so she leaned back in the bath. The water was cooling already. "Your father is despicable, and he's here and talking to our kids. I don't want him here, Andy. He makes me feel as if I'm worthless, as if I'm nothing—as if I'm responsible for him having nothing and for you losing everything you were to inherit."

"Oh, we're not going there again." He cut her off sharply and stood up, dismissing her. It was something she hadn't been on the receiving end of for so long.

"Andy, I'm your wife, and I'm telling you how I feel, how he made me feel. You can't honestly tell me you didn't see it, or maybe you didn't want to see it. This is my house, and I can't remember anyone ever making me feel as if I was an unwelcome guest. Your father is still here, and right now, the way I'm seeing you, I can tell you've bought whatever it is he's dishing out hook, line, and sinker. To make it worse, you're trying to explain that boys will be boys. Your dad has always treated women terribly, but I'm supposed to…what, just shake it off, paste a smile to my face, and say, okay, I'll let it go? No! No fucking goddamn way. We've raised our kids better than that."

"You've had a crappy morning," Andy said. "I mean, are you sure this isn't about your parents and that article?"

The way he cut her off, she knew his voice carried, and she wondered if anyone could hear. He closed the door to the bathroom. Maybe he knew. She could see how rattled he was, something else she rarely saw from her husband. Andy handled things, looked after everything. He argued, he was passionate, and she didn't know what she'd do without him. At the same time, there was a side of him that could be cruel. It had been a long time since she'd felt his words like a slap to her face.

He shook his head, running his hand over his face. "Sorry, I didn't mean it like that. Look, let's just table this. He's here. He doesn't know you. You know I love you, and this is about you and me and our family. Your parents, my dad, they're just…not part of our lives. Just get out of the bath and get dressed. Maybe he's changed —and don't give me that look. People do change, Laura."

She was shaking her head. "Andy, your father would just as soon see me out of your life. He even said it, not in so many words, when he said you chose me even when you had so many better options. Like, how do you expect me to feel?"

She unplugged the tub and stood up, and Andy held out a towel as she stepped out of the bath. He allowed his gaze to linger on her, appreciative and possessive, letting her know with just that look that she was his. He wrapped the towel around her, and she dried herself off before tucking the edge in at her breasts and taking in the way he stared down at her. Then he glanced away, considered, and nodded.

"What do you want me to do, ask him to leave?" he said.

She almost said yes before she realized it could be something that came between them down the road.

"No," she said. "Fine, I get it. I'll get dressed, come on out, paste a smile to my face, and listen to your dad go on and on. But hear me, Andy. I won't be treated like a servant or like I'm an unwanted guest in my own house, and if he says one more, cruel, demeaning…"

He touched her, his hand on her shoulder, squeezing, supporting, and then he ran it over her collarbone, her chin, her cheek. "Then he'll be out of here," he said and leaned in to press a kiss to her lips, a kiss that lingered, a kiss that reassured.

She looped her arms over his shoulders, around his neck, as she went on her tiptoes. He pulled her right against him so she could feel all his hardness. It was a place where she fit, where she felt loved, and he was giving her the reassurance she hadn't realized she needed. When he stepped back and kissed her again, her towel slipped. There was that teasing smile as his hand touched the doorknob and hers gripped the towel.

"See you out there," he said. Then he was off, and she took in the way he walked with the most perfect ass she'd ever seen before he stepped out and closed the bedroom door.

Out of nowhere, again, it seemed as if she'd forgotten to breathe.

CHAPTER
Five

"Andy, you really have one of the nicest and best-looking brood of kids I've ever seen. Every one of you gets it all from your grandfather," Todd said. He laughed again, and so did the kids. "You've done well. Looking at the legacy you've created makes me damn proud you're my son. These are my grandkids, my blood, my family."

Todd Friessen actually had his arm looped around Sara, who was beaming under all his charm, which he'd been laying on extra thick. Jeremy was leaning against the fridge, Zac standing off to the side, and Andy was pouring his dad a glass of what she knew was bourbon from the bottle that hadn't been opened since Jeremy's New Year's wedding over a year ago—and there it was, not even noon.

"Here you go, Dad." Andy offered him the glass. She noted it was the good crystal, which they never used except for holidays and special occasions, never for when someone just came over. She wanted to pull Andy aside, give him a good shake, and ask him what the hell he was doing.

"Grandma, I want a cookie." Brandon bounced into the kitchen again, and she wasn't sure if it was from everyone's excitement or from all the cookies he'd eaten—likely from the sugar he'd been pounding down, since she'd been in over her head, trying to deal with a situation she still hadn't managed to wrap her brain around.

Her parents, Todd, and the letter! She felt a flutter again in her chest and turned to the sink, resting her hands there, feeling suffocated. She had to remind herself yet again to breathe. It came out like a wheeze, and she wondered whether anyone heard.

"Hey, Brandon, no way," Jeremy said. "Geeze, Mom, how many has he had?"

She turned and stared at Jeremy, because it seemed from the way he'd just spoken to her as if he'd picked up on some of how Todd thought of her. But that was crazy. She couldn't remember ever having given her son such a disapproving glare.

"Brandon, no more cookies," she said a lot more sharply than she'd planned. "Grandma is making lunch. Jeremy, you can help." She rested her hand on the loaf of bread and gave it a shove across the island, then gestured to her son. "Grab a knife. Spread mayo on half, mustard on the other, and pull the leftover roast from the fridge."

She wondered for a second what he was going to say, but he must have realized she wasn't in the mood to play any games, as he nodded. Brandon wrapped his arm around her leg and stuck out his bottom lip to pout, and she rested her hand on his dark hair and ruffled it. "Go clean up your toys, and then we're having lunch." She patted his back, and he bumped against her once as if ready to argue but then hopped away. He never walked; he ran, he bounced, he rolled.

"Hey, Zac, you too. Give your mom a hand," Andy added, resting his hand on her bare arm. She knew he hadn't missed the fact that she was wearing the white sleeveless blouse she wore only for going out, along with beige capris. For no reason she could explain, she'd even added a hint of blush and mascara. "You look nice," he said. "Can I pour you a glass of wine?"

Had he seriously just asked that?

"Andy, it's not even noon yet. I think tea would be better—and don't you still have the cattle to move? You were barely out there before your father showed up and interrupted the morning. Then there's Brandon. Jeremy, you still need to take him over to Tiffy's parents, and don't you have to work at the hardware store at two?" She took in everyone, letting her gaze land finally on Jeremy as he reached for a beer from the fridge and cracked it open. Just because a grandfather had shown up, it was suddenly party time? She stared at the beer and gave everything to him in that one look, just daring him to lift the can and take a swallow. He must have got it, as she saw the hesitation, the way a lump worked in his throat.

"Right," he said. "I guess I thought Brandon could stay here and get to know his great-grandfather, and I'd call in and see if Cady would take my shift for me…"

Laura was already shaking her head. "I think not. You have a responsibility, and Tiffy's parents are expecting Brandon. Fair is fair. And drinking before work, this early in the day, isn't happening."

Jeremy looked over to Andy. Did he seriously think

he'd overrule her? She curled her fingers around the lip of the counter, having to fight the urge to walk over and give his ear a yank. At least he set the beer down on the counter.

"Your mother's right, Jeremy," Todd said. "A young lad has responsibilities. Even your dad, growing up, was always a big help to me. We'll have more time to get to know each other, I promise."

She gave everything to Todd, who smiled down at Sara and then at Zac and Brandon before letting his gaze linger on Jeremy. He was looking at his grandson with pride. It was a look she didn't want to see, and she found herself dragging her gaze over to Andy, who was taking in the scene. Why wasn't he saying anything, doing something to stop this madness?

"So, Dad, it's a surprise and all that you dropped by, but how long are you planning on being out this way?" Andy said.

There. Finally.

Laura reached for a cutting board and took in Jeremy, who had the bread on the island and was putting the mayo and mustard on as she'd asked. She reached in the fridge for a block of marble cheese and a head of lettuce, then spotted the pickles at the back. She reached for the jar.

"Oh, I'd like to stick around and get to know my grandkids for a while, so no plans on time or anything."

Laura pulled back and nearly dropped the jar. Sara was still taking in everything, and Zac too. He didn't even have his head buried in his phone. What the hell did Todd mean by that?

"So you have a place nearby," she said. She couldn't

help herself and didn't miss the way Andy glanced at her. But she was having none of that.

"Well, no. Was going to find a motel, a cheap one, and see about getting a room. Didn't have a chance to find someplace, as I came right here once I decided. It's been too long, too many years, and there's something about family. When you drift apart and things are said, you realize all that stuff is just that, because family is more important. I've missed too many years. Didn't get to see my grandkids grow up, offer my wisdom. Why, kids need to have their grandfather around to talk to, especially when they're growing up and have differences with their parents. But then, you kids look like you've done just fine. That doesn't surprise me, considering your dad. He always had my back in some of the worst times, you know. And two granddaughters? I'm a lucky man." He smiled and squeezed Sara tighter to him before he let her go. She beamed. Todd didn't even bother looking Laura's way as he glanced over to Andy and said, "So when do I get to meet Chelsea?"

Laura put the jar on the counter and set the lettuce and cheese in front of Jeremy. "Cut up the cheese, too, and put some lettuce on the sandwiches," she ordered.

Jeremy stilled. Of course, he had to have picked up on her mood: pissed, irritated, and pushed to the limit.

"Ah, Chels doesn't live here," Andy said. "She's married and lives in Boston with her husband, Ric." He sounded so reasonable, but she wanted to tell him to stop sharing so much about the kids. This was his father, not a man to be reasonable and have a polite conversation with.

"Sara, you said Devon was picking you up," Laura said. "You're not even dressed or ready yet. You need to go shake a leg. Zac, put some plates out on the table and grab the paper towels over there." Yup, she wasn't in a nice, pleasant mom mood, and she was sure the kids picked up on her tone.

"Can't we just grab a sandwich and eat like we always do?" Zac said. "Why do we have to sit at the table? We never do that for lunch."

Something about her kids questioning her in front of Todd wasn't working for her. She stared at Zac with a hard look. He had to know she was pushed as far as she was going to be.

"Your mom wants to sit at the table, Zac. You heard her," Andy added, then dragged his gaze over to her. She didn't miss the same question in his eyes, the teasing smile as if he was trying to get her to relax.

"So, Grandpa…"

"Grandfather. Call me Grandfather, Sara, all of you," Todd interrupted.

Laura reached for a knife and the block of cheese, as Jeremy hadn't even finished the roast beef, still slicing it and putting it on the bread. She squeezed the handle and reached for a cutting board.

Her daughter laughed, and Laura shot her a sharp glance. She needed to pull her daughter aside and have a talk with her, with all the kids, but at the same time, how much did she want to share? How much did Andy want to share? Neither had wanted their kids to know about everything Todd and Caroline had done.

"I should get ready," Sara said, and Laura inclined her head, the word *Really?* on the tip of her tongue, pure sarcasm. Sara backed up and then headed down the hall. Zac was setting the table, and Jeremy seemed to be confused about how to put together a sandwich.

"Seriously, Jeremy, does Tiffy have this much trouble with you, too?" She nudged him aside and put the cheese, lettuce, and beef on the sandwiches, quickly assembling them.

"That's not funny, Mom," he said. "Tiffy and I share the cooking. In fact, I do more than she does."

She wanted to roll her eyes, and maybe Jeremy knew. He went to reach for the beer on the counter, but Laura grabbed it first and dumped it in the sink. "Go and get Brandon washed up for lunch," she ordered, knowing Todd was still watching her.

"You shouldn't stay in a hotel, Grandfather," Zac said. "We have room. Mom, can't Grandfather stay in the spare room?"

She heard the door, the footsteps, and took in Gabriel as he stepped into the kitchen. He wore blue jeans and a faded T-shirt, his dark hair freshly cut. He took in Todd and shifted his glance to her, then Andy. He said nothing.

"Hi," she said. "Didn't know you were dropping by."

Andy lifted his hand. "Dad, you remember Gabriel."

Todd looked over to her son, and she wondered whether Gabriel remembered the estate, living there under Todd and Caroline. Of course he did. He dragged his gaze from Zac, to Jeremy, to Andy, and then to her.

"Oh, right," Todd said. "Laura's little son, who didn't talk. Wow, you're all grown up."

Her heart pounded, and she pulled in a breath, her chest rising and falling. She saw the way Jeremy and Zac looked at Gabriel with confusion. They didn't know.

"It's been a long time," Gabriel said, letting his gaze linger on Todd. "So what's going on here? Thought you were moving the cattle. Figured I'd find you out in the field." He looked over to Andy.

She could say something, but what?

"After lunch, we'll move them," Andy said.

"And Grandfather can stay here, right, Mom, Dad?" Zac asked.

She wondered by Jeremy's face whether he'd figured out yet that something wasn't quite right, as he fell unusually quiet just as Brandon came running back into the kitchen.

Hell, no. It was on the tip of her tongue. "I'm sure your grandfather would be more comfortable in a motel, Zac."

"Mom, you never let anyone stay in a hotel, and Grandfather is family."

Why wasn't Andy jumping in?

"It'll be only a few days," Todd said, "and it would be nice to be close to the kids, to my son." It was as if he'd figured out that the final decision came down to her. He had to hate that.

Andy glanced over to her and then the kids. "Sure, Dad, a few days," he said.

She turned to look at him, wondering what he was doing. Zac was saying something and laughing with Todd, and the next thing she realized, Todd had him walking out of the kitchen with him to get his bags. Laura forced herself to put down the knife. Gabriel looked from her to Andy and hadn't said a word.

"Are you kidding, Andy?" she snapped. "You invited him to stay. What are you thinking?"

"It's only a few days. I promise he'll behave himself, and if he does anything, I promise you I'll ask him to leave."

She made a rude noise and took in Gabriel, who glanced over his shoulder and then back to them, then shook his head.

Andy leaned against the island, sliding his arm out and pulling her close. "What are you worried about?" he said.

She stepped closer and rested her arms on his forearms. "Everything, Andy. You just invited a snake into a henhouse."

Andy pulled her close, pressed a kiss to her forehead, and then stepped away. "Maybe once upon a time, but he's lost everything, Laura, and sometimes when that happens to someone, they turn into a better person."

She wondered if he really believed that. She glanced over to Gabriel, who she could see was holding something back. Yeah, he remembered. How could he not?

"I'm going to go give Zac a hand," Andy said, then stepped out of the kitchen, Brandon heading after him. That left her, Gabriel, and Jeremy.

"You think he wants something?" Gabriel asked, and she didn't miss the shock in Jeremy's expression as he stared at him.

"Don't know," she replied, "but this is Todd Friessen, and there's one thing I know about him: We can't take anything at face value. He wants something, he's up to something, and whatever it is could end up costing this family in ways I don't think any of us can imagine."

"Maybe…" Gabriel started.

"Evidently, there's something about him I don't know," Jeremy finally said.

When she heard the door close again, cutting off the voices of Todd, Andy, Zac, and Brandon, Laura rested her hand on Jeremy's arm. "Yeah," she said. "Just do me a favor. Make sure no one is ever alone with him."

Jeremy's eyes widened.

"You want me to have a word with Dad?" Gabriel asked, but she just shook her head as she listened to Andy laugh.

"No, I'll talk to him."

But what could she say? She needed to talk some sense into Andy and try to figure out why he was suddenly welcoming a man into their home who'd tried to destroy their family and separate her from her children—all because of money, power, and position.

CHAPTER
Six

"Do you want me to stay?" Gabriel said as he leaned on the kitchen island, where Laura was shucking corn for dinner. Ribs and baked potatoes were in the oven, and she was thinking of coleslaw instead of a tossed salad, depending on how much trouble she wanted to go to.

She was lost in her head still, having accomplished nothing since everyone had left after the sandwiches and Todd's two shots of bourbon. She couldn't believe he'd then gotten on a horse or that Andy had let him.

"No, go," she said. "You don't need to hang around for my benefit. Besides, I thought Elizabeth had some dinner thing for you and her family tonight?"

She took in the ring on Gabriel's finger. His hands were still dirty from helping with the herd, which Andy had decided to do after lunch. What had his father done but insist on helping? She wasn't sure why her husband had seemed inclined to let him tag along.

As she took in Gabriel, she realized there would always be an indescribably strong bond between them, a different bond than she had with her other children. It was just that they'd been through hell and back together and experienced the kind of hardships very few did. The two of them had been living hand to mouth, struggling for the basics that many took for granted—but that had been before Andy.

It was humbling to remember, yet here she was with a life and a family she'd never expected. At the same time, she would never forget where she came from.

"Not really a family dinner," Gabriel said. "Just her brother, Marty, is coming over. He has a new girlfriend and wants us to meet her during, you know, a relatively sane and quiet dinner. I think he wants her approval, but he wants to introduce her to Elizabeth's family in small doses and not have her running for the hills after meeting the rest of the Abercrombies. They're an acquired taste."

Hearing Gabriel's references to Elizabeth's absurd and unusual family always brought a smile to her face. There was something about the Abercrombies that was so out there, so unusual. They never would've been invited to a dinner with Andy's parents, who would've been horrified by the spectacle, but at the same time, the Abercrombies were good people. Though they were a little loud, obnoxious, and rough around the edges, she'd definitely rather rub shoulders with them than with those in Todd Friessen's world.

"Enjoy," she said. "No, don't cancel. If you ask me, it sounds as if you have the better deal. Besides, I'm not about to let the likes of Todd Friessen chase me out of my own house. Did he really help with moving the cattle?" She was having trouble with the image, considering she didn't think he owned a pair of cowboy boots or could remember how to sit on a horse and get his hands dirty. His dress shoes, she'd noticed, were completely inappropriate for riding.

"Wouldn't say he helped much. It was more me and Zac and Dad who did everything, being short Jeremy and Sara, but Dad loaned him a pair of his older boots. He saddled him on Chelsea's horse, and he at least stayed enough out of the way that he didn't cause too much of a disruption. He didn't do any tricks, but nevertheless, he seemed to be trying to impress Zac."

She lifted her gaze and let it linger, wondering what Gabriel was hinting at.

He shrugged just as she heard voices outside, then inclined his head. "You know, showing off how impressive and important he is," he clarified. "He was talking about growing up with Rodney—the old place, he kept calling it. Talked about the herds they'd moved, their time in the saddle, and he even referred a number of times to how his brother had inherited all the property, and here he is, a pauper."

She was still staring in horror as she heard the screen door squeak, bringing in Zac's excited chatter. At the same time, she heard a car pulling in, and Gabriel glanced out the window and said, "Sara and Devon are here. This should be interesting."

Andy strode into the kitchen, Todd behind him, talking about cattle prices and some new herd he should be looking at, or maybe it was some investment he should consider. She was still reeling, trying to figure out why this day had turned into the disaster it was.

Andy kissed her forehead when she looked up, and she took in his teasing smile. He pressed a kiss to her lips then, and it wasn't lost on her how unusually happy he seemed. She still wanted to pull him aside and ask what he was thinking, allowing Todd to linger, to stay there, and to get anywhere near their kids and spend any time with them.

"Dinner smells great," Andy said. "I'm starving. When are we eating?"

"Half hour, give or take. So how did it go? You moved all the cattle?" she asked, doing her best to ignore Todd, who was lurking in the kitchen, saying nothing, though she knew he was watching her and Andy. The tension spiked as he took in Gabriel. Andy had to notice, right? But he was now washing his hands at the kitchen sink, his back to them.

Zac walked in, and Todd lit up, directing his smile and charm his way as they started talking. The ease, the comfort…yeah, he didn't see Gabriel as his grandson. No, both she and Gabriel were outsiders, misfits.

"Not all," Andy said. "Need to find the stragglers in the morning."

"You don't need me tomorrow, do you, Dad?" Gabriel asked, and Todd looked over from where he was talking with Zac.

"No, but this weekend we need to separate some of the calves. Bring Elizabeth and Shaunty out, and we'll make a day of it. We'll barbecue some burgers," Andy said.

Gabriel started out of the kitchen just as Sara and Devon strode in. Devon was in blue jeans and a white and black tee with a jean jacket overtop, and Sara was looking casual but stylish in flat boots that went to her knees, a light brown skirt, and a paisley blouse.

"Just in time for dinner," Laura said. "Devon, are you joining us tonight?"

Devon had his arm looped around Sara's shoulders. He was so damn tall and charming, so handsome. Gabriel paused on his way out, and she knew he was waiting to see how Todd would react to Devon.

"Not tonight," Devon replied. "I have to work—but another time." He leaned down and kissed Sara, and she didn't miss Andy's expression as he dried his hands and gestured toward them with his chin. She knew he was having trouble with Sara dating. Todd was too, evidently; though she couldn't hear what he was saying to Zac, she didn't miss the way he was watching Devon.

"Great to see you, Devon," Andy said.

"You too, Mr. and Mrs. Friessen," Devon said.

It brought a smile to her face. He was always so damn polite, and she really liked him for Sara. She was positive Andy did, too, even though she knew he'd never admit it, considering Sara was his baby girl.

"Oh, Devon, this is my grandfather," Sara said before Devon could leave, and Laura could feel Andy behind her as she watched the exchange.

Todd shook Devon's hand. "It's a pleasure, Devon. So you're dating my granddaughter?" he said. Just his tone had Laura's back going up, as he sounded so presumptuous, as if he had a say in the matter.

"Yes, sir, I am." Devon pulled his hand away, and she wondered at the way Todd was looking at him, the heavy gaze. His smile softened as it landed on Sara. She didn't know what he would say.

"Well, I'm sure I'll be seeing you again, then," he finally said—as if he suddenly thought he would be sticking around! Yeah, no. She'd definitely be having a word with Andy that night.

Devon didn't respond, just glanced over his shoulder to her and Andy.

"Sorry about the third degree, Devon," Laura said. "Andy's father isn't staying long."

Todd stilled. Yeah, he'd felt the shot.

Devon crooked his brow as if he understood what she was saying. "Okay, goodnight, y'all," he said, then started out of the kitchen.

"Devon, I'll walk you out," Sara added.

Laura knew it would likely be a long goodbye on the other side of the porch, where Andy wouldn't be able to see them wrapped in each other's arms. She picked up the butcher knife and rested the cabbage on the cutting board.

"Well, you surprise me, Andy," Todd said after Sara and Devon had left. She wasn't sure what Todd meant, but there was something in his tone.

"Why's that, Dad?" Andy replied.

Todd allowed his gaze to drift over to Laura first, and she glanced over to Zac, who was leaning off to the side, on his phone. "I was going to say *Guess Who's Coming to Dinner*, but that's a little before your time. Can't believe you're allowing a darkie to put his hands on your daughter."

Laura felt the jab as she nicked her finger, too stunned over what Todd had just said to pay attention to the cabbage. "Ah, shit," she hissed, pressing at the dripping blood, yet she was still rooted to the spot.

"Excuse me?" Andy said. His tone held shock and something else, an edge.

Maybe Todd knew, as he lifted his hands, but he made no excuse. Apparently he was also a racist along with being the scourge of the earth.

Andy had a hold of her hand then and held it under the water, rinsing away the blood. It was careless, not something she'd ever done before. She knew the knife had likely slipped because of her shock. In fact, she was still reeling.

"I just mean that I can't believe you're letting your daughter date someone who isn't her kind," Todd said.

Andy was standing so close now that she couldn't look over her shoulder. The way he held her hand under the water, she could feel his tension. Good. Maybe he'd show his dad the door.

When Andy stepped back and reached for a paper towel, she turned off the water and glanced over to Zac. His expression was one of confusion or shock, or likely a mix of both.

"Sara is dating a very good and decent young man who makes her very happy," Andy said, handing Laura the paper towel. "You need to watch yourself, Dad. That kind of racism isn't welcome in my house."

Laura wrapped the towel around her finger, seeing and feeling the tension that now lingered between father and son.

"Sorry, didn't mean any disrespect," Todd said and lifted his hands again.

She heard the screen door slap closed as a car started up, and Sara's smiling face as she walked in confirmed that she didn't have a clue what her grandfather thought of the young man who'd saved her, whom she was completely, head-over-heels in love with.

At least one good thing had come out of the exchange, though: Andy was suddenly on guard again. Maybe he'd just realized that allowing Todd to be there wasn't such a great idea, after all.

L aura ran lotion over her dry legs as she sat on the bench at the foot of their queen bed, a towel wrapped around her. She'd decided to have yet another bath before bed to try to soak out the heaviness that had settled into her shoulders from the shittiness of the day.

She still hadn't made any sense of everything: her asshole parents, Andy's father (who was still there), and the letter. Damn! She still hadn't had a chance to show Andy that letter, which meant just one more person was messing with her.

She took in the closed door, the light wood bed frame, and the matching bedroom suite, with dressers and nightstands. The two closets were on Andy's list to renovate, as they wanted something larger, a walk-in. She loved this house, but at the same time, the sprawling west coast rancher was beginning to show its age.

There was something about the house at night, when everyone was settling in. It had become her favorite part of the day, except that night there was an unwelcome guest at the end of the hall, staying in the guest room—or rather, what had been Chelsea's bedroom. She wanted time alone with Andy to find out where his head was at and what the hell he was thinking, letting his father stay under their roof.

She rubbed in the remaining lotion, hearing the murmur of voices in the distance, a door closing, footsteps. Then the bedroom door opened, and Andy stepped in.

It was in that one look he gave her, the intensity in his expression, in his eyes. At one time, what had seemed so much like darkness lurking in him had scared the shit out of her, but that had been before she understood him, before she knew him on the level she did now. With his deep, difficult personality, she now understood he struggled with overthinking everything, with always trying to protect them.

"You had another bath," he finally said, sounding distracted. Then he turned away and untucked his shirt from his jeans, pulled it over his head, and tossed it on the bed. He sat at the edge and pulled off his boots, letting out a breath that sounded more like a groan. Yeah, he was tense. She could always tell.

"You could've joined me," she said. Sharing a bath or a shower was something they did to connect, but not tonight.

"My dad wanted to talk to me," he replied. Then he didn't say anything else, just stood up. His gaze lingered on her as he unbuckled his belt and undressed, then walked naked into the bathroom. She listened to the shower and took in the closed bedroom door.

She stood up, her hand going to the V of her breasts, where the towel was tucked, and strode into the bathroom. Andy was in the shower already, washing his hair under the spray. His hand was against the wall, but he wasn't at ease. No, she could see some lingering tension, and for some reason, it reminded her of who he used to be before severing ties with his family years ago. That had changed him into the man he was today, but having Todd Friessen back, an interloper, a horrible man who she knew without a doubt had an agenda… Nothing good could ever come of having a man like Todd Friessen around.

"So what did your dad want to talk to you about?" she said. "You can't just drop a bomb like that and then not tell me what's going on. Why is he still here, Andy?"

She wondered if he hadn't realized she'd followed him into the bathroom, by the way he turned to look at her through the glass shower wall. He rinsed the soap off his body and didn't say anything for the longest time. Then he turned off the shower and stepped out, and she reaching for the towel on the rack, shook it out, and handed it to him. His gaze reached out to her—dark, mistrusting, simmering. Why?

"He lost everything," he replied. "He said that being alone for so many years gave him an epiphany. He was so alone, with no close family, and he just doesn't want to die alone. That's where he sees his life heading. He's getting older, and he wants to know me, our kids, his grandkids…" Andy pulled in a breath and ran the towel over his hair, his legs, his back. "It seems mending fences, so to speak, is why he's here. He wants to make things right."

It was the way Andy said it that concerned her. He glanced to her as he folded the towel and looped it once again over the rack, and for a minute, it hit her that maybe he really did believe that. But how?

"I can see by your face that you're horrified," he said. "I know he treated you like crap. You have a right to be angry, to be suspicious, but at the same time, people change."

Was he serious? She crossed her arms, gripping the edge of the towel. "How can you believe that? You're saying that even after tonight, with the way he spoke about Devon? Your dad, along with being a shitty person, is a racist. You can't seriously believe that he's changed. You know, Andy, I understand better than anybody why you would want to think your dad is different, but he made it very clear when the twins were young and Sara was a baby, before Zac was born, that he wanted position, power, money, and I was in the way. I had to go.

"You know that, and you know he was only going to get all that through your birthright. But there was me, and don't forget Gabriel, standing in his way because I'm married to you. Let me give you a little refresher, in case you missed it earlier tonight in the kitchen: Your dad wants nothing to do with Gabriel. He tells the kids to call him Grandfather, but not Gabriel. He'll never accept him. You know that. I mean, on horseback, Andy, did he in any way try to have a conversation with Gabriel or treat him like he was his grandson?"

Andy said nothing, and she could see him thinking, see his anger.

Before he could answer, she cut in and said, "No, he

didn't. And then there's me. He hates me, he blames me, and I understand from Gabriel that he talked Zac's head off about what a pauper he is. I mean, what the hell is that about, trying to make the kids feel sorry for him? Andy, come on…"

She knew she was ranting, and she could see how uptight Andy was. He was getting his back up, just listening to what she was saying.

He let out a breath, and it sounded so much like frustration. "You may be reading too much into it. You know there's a lot of history between us, and I know he treated you horribly, and you may be thinking he's going to repeat that history, but I did have a chance to talk with my dad, and he told me he regrets how he treated you, that he wants to make amends. He said he's happy for me, happy that I have you and our family and our kids in this life that I've carved out for us. He's proud of me, and he wants to make things right, Laura. My dad has always been rough around the edges, but I think him coming here and making the effort says something."

For a minute, Laura didn't know what to say. Andy ran his hand through his wet hair and walked out of the bathroom, still naked. He'd always been so comfortable in his body, and she took in his amazing ass and the muscles that bunched in his back as he strode around the bed and pulled back the duvet. The bedside light was on, and he climbed into bed and propped the pillows behind him.

She just stared, because she couldn't believe he could be that naive. That was something he never did. Andy Friessen was realistic beyond realistic, seeing the bad side and planning for the worst. He never gave the benefit of the doubt to someone who'd done him wrong. This was not a side of Andy she'd ever seen.

"Look, I'm tired," he said. "Let's talk about this tomorrow. Let's just get some sleep." He ran his hand over his face, and she listened to the scrape of whiskers.

Laura pulled the damp towel free and dumped it in the hamper before walking to the bed, naked, and climbing in. His gaze lingered, and she knew he loved her body even though it seemed he was brooding beside her. "No, Andy, I want to talk about this now, because I'm probably the only one who isn't seeing this situation and your father through rose-colored glasses. How he saw Devon, what he said, should have you seeing that he isn't this nice changed man you believe he is."

She knew her voice was loud, and she had to calm herself, changing it to a whisper, staring at the closed door before looking back to Andy. He pulled in another breath, and she could hear the frustration. She was pushing, but then, he was such a difficult man. If she weren't as strong as she was, she likely would have drowned under his personality.

"I hear you, Laura, and I know what he said. I had a talk with him about it, about a lot of things, about how viewing people by their separate classes, skin colors, and backgrounds doesn't work. I told him he can't do that here, and he said he understood. He apologized to me and said he didn't mean for it to come out the way it did, and he assured me it won't happen again."

"And you believe him?" She scooted down under the covers, lying down and rolling to her side.

"Look, Laura, I need you to give him the benefit of the doubt. He's trying. I need you to try, too."

For a second, she couldn't believe it. She didn't know what to say. "You want me to give your dad the benefit of the doubt? We're talking about a man who's angry with me because you lost your inheritance, all because you wouldn't leave me, because I'm not acceptable, because your dad and your mom planned for you to have this life that included the right kind, which isn't me—and now you want me to give him the benefit of the doubt?"

He had that hard, brooding look again. They were so close she could feel his breath on her face from the pillow next to her.

"Why, Andy? Why would you ask that of me? What's going on with you? Let me remind you that you wrote your dad off and got him out of your life, our lives. You made it clear he wasn't welcome here, around our children, and yet now he's sleeping under our roof, near our kids, and you're suddenly okay with it? I don't understand, Andy. What's gotten into you?" She was so angry that she rolled over on her side, giving him her back.

"You wouldn't understand, Laura. It's just…he's my dad. And I know what he did, and yes, I've been angry at him for everything for so many years, for how he treated you and how he wanted to destroy our family all because of money and power and everything. I just want to think now that he can see what we have and how wonderful our family is. And Gabriel, he's my son. I'll make sure my dad understands that."

Andy slid his arm over her and pulled himself closer to her, pressed against her under the covers, all that warmth and hardness. She loved feeling him and had to close her eyes for a second to stop herself from letting him convince her this was a good thing. It would be so easy to go along with Andy.

"Just give me some credit, Laura," he said. "I know what you're saying, but believe me when I say I know when Todd is up to something, and I don't think he is. He's got nothing, Laura, and I'm seeing a humble man who lost everything. What does he have to show for all those years of staying with my mother, a woman he despised and didn't love, just so he could have money, power, position, everything? He doesn't have any of that now. He has nothing, and his ego took a shit-kicking. Maybe he's still an asshole, but he's my father, and I want to believe he's trying and that's why he showed up on our doorstep." Andy pressed a kiss to her shoulder, and she turned around in his arms before he could take it further.

"Andy, I'm not saying I don't hope he's changed, but I think you're wrong. I mean, I would love for my parents to show up here and apologize, to try to make things right, but that's not going to happen. Look at your dad and who he is—even how he treated women, for God's sake, and how many he went through. I know what it was like because I was on the receiving end of it as a maid in that mansion, just a kid myself. I remember the way your father watched me. It was repulsive, feeling his eyes on me. He made me feel meaningless, like a sexual object for his enjoyment, and you know what? It wasn't okay, and here you have him under this roof, our roof, with our kids, who are impressionable. You want them picking up all of his rough edges? Because I sure in the hell don't."

"Enough," Andy said. He moved away, cutting her

off abruptly and tossing back the covers, furious. He got out of bed and stood there, naked.

She knew when he was angry, but then, she wasn't backing down. She really was pushing his limits.

He jammed his hands in his hair. "At least my dad is here," he said. "What does that say about your parents, Laura? I'm not saying that to hurt you, but he's here, he's trying, he's making an effort…" Andy paced, striding around the bed until he was right in front of her. "Please, Laura, meet him halfway. I know it's asking a lot, but please do this for me."

She couldn't remember having seen this kind of passion from him, though to her, it seemed to be mixed with false hope. She pulled in a breath as she stared up at him. The way he was looking at her, she could see his love, and she didn't want to say no. "You understand what you're asking, even with the way he treated me?" she said.

He sat on the bed, right beside her, in her space, and let his hand rest on her thigh. He pulled her to him and pressed a kiss to the side of her head as she leaned into him. "I will see to it that he apologizes for how he treated you."

What was she supposed to say to that? He was their protector, he loved her, and she loved him for that. She sighed in his arms. "You know I cannot ever say no to you," she said, then pulled back and looked up to him.

As he slid his hand over her cheek, in her hair, she leaned into his touch. He pressed a kiss to her lips, which she offered to him, and could feel his teasing smile as he kissed her. He pulled back but didn't let his hands fall away.

"Thank you," he said. "You know what? I think you

might be surprised to find that Todd may just be a different man."

She loved her husband so much, more than she could have ever imagined she could love a man, but as he laid her down on her back, running his hands over her in a way that left her with no doubt as to what she meant to him, she knew that where his father was concerned, Andy Friessen was wrong.

Eight

L ight was pouring in through the bedroom window when Laura woke and reached out to feel the bed empty beside her. She stretched and smiled, still feeling the closeness of the night before, the passion and the insistent need of her husband as he slipped inside her and kissed her. It had been tender and loving, and it brought her the confidence of knowing she was a well-loved woman.

Then she remembered Todd, who was there in her house, which had her throwing back the covers and tugging on a pair of sweatpants and a T-shirt. She pulled her robe on just as she threw open the door to the bedroom and took a second to listen to the sounds of the house. A glance at the clock on the dresser told her it was after eight.

She heard nothing but silence, taking in Zac and Sara's closed doors. They were evidently still in bed. Todd's was closed, too. Good, at least no one else was up. She strode down the hall, running her hands through her tangled hair, and yawned. The door was open, and she felt the breeze through the screen, knowing Andy would already be outside, feeding the herd.

"Good morning, Laura."

She jumped at his deep voice and pressed a hand to her chest. Todd was holding a mug of coffee in the kitchen. He was dressed rather sharply in a dark blue long-sleeved button-up shirt, dark blue jeans, and a leather belt, and his white hair was neat and tidy. She took in the thick gold ring on his finger and couldn't remember whether that was his wedding band. Then she remembered herself and tried to pull herself together as she yanked the edge of her housecoat closed, covering herself in front of a man she despised.

"Todd, I trust you slept well," she found herself saying as she stepped into the kitchen and saw the pot of coffee Andy had made. It brought a smile to her lips, but at the same time, she could feel the eyes of the jackal behind her burning into her.

"I did. Quaint, quiet place, this is. My son's done well for himself."

Laura reached for a mug in the cupboard and poured herself a cup. She wasn't sure what she was supposed to say to that. She lifted her mug and took a swallow, but she would have enjoyed it more if Todd hadn't been here. The way he was looking at her now, she knew without a doubt that he wasn't on the same page as Andy. He still hated her.

"Yes, well, we love our life here and our family, our children. It makes all the difference when there's love involved. Make no mistake: Andy loves me and I him. We have everything we need or want," she added.

His smile revealed his amusement. He was still a

smug bastard. "A step up for you. You did well for your-self, scoring my son. Apparently, you keep him happy." He dragged his gaze over her, down to her feet and then back up. It was the kind of look that left her feeling naked and exposed.

Where the hell was her husband? She lifted her other hand and pulled at the cloth of her housecoat, keeping it together and holding it at her chest, feeling as if she didn't belong in her own house.

"And you provided him a fine brood of kids, my grandkids," Todd continued. Then he inclined his head, and she tried to see how he could be a brother to Rodney Friessen, a man she respected, who would never treat her so poorly. He offered her another smile and said, "I'm just teasing, Laura." He rested his hand on the island, and she wondered if her shock showed on her face.

"What do you want, Todd? Why are you really here?"

He lifted his brows, and his smile disappeared. "To see my son and meet my grandkids, whom I was denied a chance to watch growing up. I suppose if Andy had taken the inheritance that was rightfully his and honored the terms of the separation from you, he may have found his way back to you. It was foolish, really, on both your parts. You could have had so much more."

Was he serious? She felt the pull in her chest again and had to remind herself to breathe. "You don't get it," she said. "That's such a shame. This isn't about money, because money can't buy a family, happiness, love. I told you already that we have everything we need. Andy didn't want that kind of life, and seeing him break away from you, from Caroline, and seeing the good, honest, decent man he is today, I doubt very much Andy would agree with you. Unlike you, Todd, Andy can't be bought. I can't be bought. We raised our children to love and respect others. So no, it was smart on Andy's part. He never for a moment considered taking that…that…" She couldn't get the words out to describe how Caroline had taken one last shot from the grave to get her out of Andy's life. She hated the woman still for all she'd tried to do, for what she'd tried to take.

Todd inhaled and glanced to the side, and it had her skin crawling. "You seem to forget, Laura, I know Andy well. There was a time in his life when we were closer than any two can be. He did things for me that made me so damn proud, and at the same time, he had my back in a way no one ever has. I admit that I did some things I'm not proud of." He gestured with his mug and took a swallow. "But I can tell you I've always been damn proud of my son, of who he is—but then, I raised him. And then he met you."

Laura stilled again, unable to lift her mug and take a swallow of the coffee that she longed for each morning. "And what? Is this where you tell me you wish he'd never met me? Is this where you try to insult me in my own house? Don't forget you're a guest here."

She listened to the rough laugh under his breath as he glanced down. What the hell was he thinking? "No, I assure you I've not forgotten you live here, considering the noises coming from Andy's bedroom last night. Brought a smile to my face. He really is a chip off the old block, and I can understand the spring in his step this morning. I did tell him not to get too attached to one woman, but would he listen?" He shook his head.

She was reeling at the fact that he was talking about

listening in on her and Andy having sex the night before. The man was disgusting, a pig.

"No, Andy has always had a piece of my brother in him, of his cousins, no matter what I did to get it out of him," Todd said. "So be it. Apparently, you make him happy."

Was that his way of giving his approval? He'd just insulted her, degraded her, and let her know he still saw her as beneath him. She wanted him gone.

"You're disgusting," she said. "I can't believe my husband let you stay."

He didn't smile this time as he rested his mug on the counter. "Andy made it clear that I need to apologize to you, and because I love my son and I want him in my life, I'm willing to lower my standards and step into the gutter and say anything, because Andy means the world to me and because my grandchildren deserve to know me, and I them. So for that reason, I will humble myself to the likes of you, a maid with an illegitimate kid, a nothing, a nobody.

"I mean, who are you, really? You're just a girl from nowhereville who was tossed out by her parents, just another statistic, another wayward pregnant teen whose prospects for a future were slim. Because I love my son, I'll say the words I can't even feel sincere about. So, Laura, I apologize if you felt slighted, even though you don't deserve my son and now have a life you should never have had. What are the chances that someone like you could live carefree and happy? No, I learned a long time ago that life isn't fair, and more often than not, people don't get what they're entitled to.

"I won't say what I really think of you," he continued. "I won't say how I wish my son will one day wake up and realize his mistake, even though it's too late for him to have what his mother willed to him, what she promised me. I won't say the one thing I've wanted to say to you for years: You owe me." He leaned in on the last part and then lifted his mug, glanced away, and sighed as if he was happy and relieved. "Well, I think I'll go out and see my son, see if I can lend him a hand." He winked at her. "You have a good morning, Laura, and enjoy the coffee that I made."

Then he walked out of the kitchen, out of the house, and Laura had to remind herself to breathe as she turned to the back door where all the mail was shoved, where that letter still was. He'd just said the three words that she knew were in that envelope. Like, holy shit! She pulled in another breath and reminded herself that at least she now knew who had sent that letter. The only problem was proving it.

"Mom, what are you doing?" Sara said.

Laura was rummaging through the mail, looking for the envelope after what Todd had said. "Sara, did you touch that letter?" she asked. Her stomach was in knots, and the few sips of coffee had burned. She'd taken the pot that Todd had apparently felt the need to make and dumped it down the drain. Damn Andy, anyway, for allowing his father there!

"No, did you show it to Dad?"

Laura took in the pile of papers as she pushed up the sleeve of her housecoat, her hair a mess, feeling gritty. "Didn't have a chance, with everything going on, with his dad showing up here and then staying. That's kind of taken a front seat to everything else." Then there was that article about her parents, which had left her feeling worthless, as if she was a nobody, with not even a mention of her existence, even though there was nothing rational about feeling the way she did.

"Mm, maybe Dad picked it up," Sara said. "You

know how he is, going through this stuff, or maybe Jeremy…" She moved beside Laura and started rummaging through the papers.

Laura had started making a pile of junk mail, garbage, and bills they needed to set up online to go paperless. After all, it was now the twenty-first century. She didn't think Andy had seen it, though, because if he had, he'd have been in her face, asking her what the hell it was. She suspected it was Todd, and it was starting to make a lot of sense. Wasn't this right up his alley? It would've been up Caroline's, for sure. The two had always been on the same page regarding how to screw someone over.

"You know, we need to have a talk about your grandfather," Laura said as she took in the papers Sara continued to sift through. She hoped Sara would be able to find the letter, but at the same time, she already knew it wasn't there anymore.

Sara glanced over and frowned. "I think it's so cool, him showing up here and staying around. I just wish Devon had been able to stay. I'm sure Grandfather would've loved to get to know him. He said as much last night, with the questions he asked about Devon. It's just…" Sara shrugged, and Laura was horrified by the joy she saw on her face.

"Oh, what questions? I didn't know he spoke with you last night," she said. She'd been exhausted from all the stress, keeping her eyes on Zac as Todd talked with him, and then with Tiffy as she popped in for just a second, and then with Sara. He'd seemed to be in his element, talking to everyone, laughing, joking, even having serious conversations with everyone who wasn't her.

"Yeah, when Dad was helping you with the dishes, Grandfather pulled me aside and asked me about Devon, how we met, who his family is, what he does for a living, if Dad has met his parents," Sara said. "It wasn't until he asked about his background that I had to laugh and tell him to lighten up. I told him Dad had already scared the ever-living crap out of Devon and any guy who came to the door, making it clear that if he hurt me in any way, he'd kill him."

She stared at Sara, feeling the bite of anger. Where did Todd get the nerve? Hadn't Andy said he'd told his dad to back off? She couldn't figure out what his game was. "That's totally inappropriate," she replied. "It's none of his business who you're seeing, and let me be clear, Sara: Todd Friessen has no say in this house, or over you or Zac or any of us. He's a guest here and needs to know his place. I hope you didn't share anything about Devon with him."

Sara was giving her the oddest look. "Well, not really. I laughed because I thought he was teasing and told him that Dad had already taken care of letting Devon know that he didn't get a free pass. Well, that's what Devon told me. There's just times with Devon when he pulls back and sets boundaries, saying he doesn't want to get on Dad's bad side."

"And your grandfather just let it drop, right?" She didn't know why, but she wanted to know every single thing Todd had said.

Sara frowned, and the way she furrowed her brow reminded Laura so much of Andy, even though at times looking at Sara was like looking at her own younger self in a mirror. "Well, sort of," Sara said. "We had a good laugh over Dad, and Grandfather said he was glad to hear that Dad is being so vigilant and that it was something he learned from him. Then he did say something odd, which I kind of chalked up to his generation."

She stopped talking, and Laura wanted to reach out and shake her daughter. "Sara, what? Come on, spill."

"Well, he said he considered it his job to keep an eye on me and make sure I have everything that can be afforded to me. He told me how important it is at my age not to be too serious with Devon, to take things slow, to have fun, and that seriousness is something that will come down the road with someone who can provide me the kind of life I'm entitled to. I thought it was kind of weird, considering, because he talked about cotillions and about meeting the right sort, and about going to college, and then he mentioned introducing me to the right kind of families, to a senator's son. But don't worry, Mom. I'm not taking him seriously."

At Sara's teasing expression, Laura wondered if her face showed how sick to her stomach she felt. So Todd was still playing games. "Well, that's totally inappropriate, Sara. Todd had no business interfering with you and Devon—and, for the record, I think Devon is good and decent. The 'right sort' that your grandfather is referring to has nothing to do with goodness or decency and why two people should be together. He's all about money, power. Sara, your grandfather has always seen marriage as a business merger."

Sara dumped the pile of papers on the counter again, took in Laura, and made a rude noise. "Well, let him," she said. "Give me a little more credit, Mom. I'm not interested in letting Grandfather set me up with some rich blueblood. Besides, I'm just glad Devon didn't stay, because he wouldn't have taken too kindly to some of the things Grandfather said."

She couldn't get her tongue to move. Maybe that was why Sara reached over and touched her arm, taking in her housecoat and her dishevelled look. Sara was in a tank top and sweats, the same things she slept in every night. "He's having a little trouble with the fact that Devon is black and I'm white," she finally said. "You think I don't know when someone is racist even though they adamantly deny it? I see it often, Mom, and not just from Grandfather—who, by the way, did his best to overcompensate. At the same time, Mom, I tried to explain to Grandfather that I don't see color in anyone. I see who they are. He didn't seem to get that, but it doesn't matter if he does, because you and Dad do. But you're right about the letter, Mom. It's not here." Sara inhaled and tapped her fingers on the counter.

Laura was stuck on the wise words of her daughter, something she'd not expected. "Well….good," was all she could get out. "So I'll ask your dad about the letter. Maybe he did grab it. And hey, before you take off, let me just tell you how proud I am of you."

Sara lifted a brow, teasing. Though Laura knew Sara had a great head on her shoulders and was confident and strong minded and stubborn just like her father, she was still surprised by how mature she sounded. She had the kind of confidence that wouldn't allow anyone to sway her in her beliefs. "Okay, Mom, so how long do you think Dad's dad is going to be staying with us?"

"I don't know for sure, Sara, but hopefully not more than a few days. You okay with that?" She asked, hoping for yes but fearing she'd say no.

Sara shrugged. "Sure, it'll be great to get to know

him, to get to know what makes Dad tick and get grumpy at times, to learn why he is the way he is. I always wondered about Dad's other side, since neither of you is great at sharing. You always say it's best this way, and sometimes it's best not to have family in your life. At least now I have a picture in my head."

She didn't know what to say to that. "A picture?"

"You know how some people come from underprivileged backgrounds and have seen the worst of life, and it makes them better people? Then there are some who come from an overprivileged world but are still lonely hearts. Grandfather clearly comes from privilege, so I guess it's a wonder that Dad turned out as well as he did. Maybe he has you to thank?" Sara said, her tone teasing. She stopped at the coffeemaker and pulled out the carafe, then said, "I would have thought there would be coffee already."

Laura started to say something as she watched her daughter make a fresh pot, but instead she shrugged before tucking all the papers back into the slots, wondering whether Todd was behind the letter. Maybe he was the one who'd taken it. "Hey, Sara, do me a favor," she added.

Her daughter's familiar green eyes stared back at her. "Yeah?"

"Don't say anything about the letter to anyone until I have a chance to talk to your dad."

Sara nodded. "Okay, but when you do talk to Dad, let me know, because I'm dying to see his reaction." Then she laughed as she strode out of the kitchen. At times, she had the oddest sense of humor.

Well, at least Laura didn't have to worry about Sara with Todd. Evidently, she'd done a great job with her daughter. Not only was she gorgeous and kind, but she had a great head on her shoulders.

She'd also finally realized what her worry was, and it was one she hadn't felt in a long time. She hadn't been willing to admit that what had been bothering her about Todd was that he could possibly come between her and her family.

"What are you doing?"

Laura hadn't heard Andy come in, and she jumped from where she sat in his leather chair behind his desk, her hand on the mouse. She was still staring at the computer screen, reading that damn article about her parents on the front page of a magazine called *Christian New Beginning*.

Her hair was damp from the shower, and she found herself looking beyond Andy to see if there was anyone with him—namely his father. "Oh, you know, attacking one problem after another. I came in here to look for a missing envelope, thinking you moved it, since you often go through the mail in the kitchen slot. Then I saw your computer on and Googled my parents' article, and, like with a five-car pile-up, I couldn't not look. It was calling me. I figured I've been far too happy lately and need to have my ego knocked down a peg or two."

She took in his amused expression, which seemed a little pained, as he strode around and rested his butt on the desk right there in her space. She groaned as she leaned back in his leather chair. Her red long-sleeved shirt molded around her generous C cups, and she also wore comfortable lowriders, her bare feet shoved in fleece-lined moccasins. She rested her hand on Andy's thigh and rubbed.

He took in the screen and the article before sliding his gaze back on her. She already knew what he was going to say as she ran her hand over his knee and just looked at him. "Why are you punishing yourself by reading this again?" he said, then actually powered off the screen. She wondered if he had any idea that his simple solution by no means removed the article from her mind. It was stuck there on an auto loop.

"Okay, maybe I'm into being a masochist," she said. "It's not that easy to get it out of my head, though. It hurts to be thought of as nothing, as if I could so easily be tossed away, even though you and I both know what they did was horrible. If it was Sara, even though we would've pulled up the drawbridge around her—that is, after you killed the boy who got her pregnant—we nevertheless would have loved her, protected her. She would've been here with the baby. We wouldn't have tossed her out of the house as if she were nothing, as my parents did, or treated her as horribly as I was. But even though I know that, Andy, I still can't help feeling that I did something despicable that made me less of a person and not worthy of their love." She tapped his leg when he pulled in a breath, ready to tell her she was being ridiculous. "And before you tell me not to think like that, that they're the ones in the wrong, I know that. All the same, please understand there's still a piece of me that can't shake the voice that creeps up out of nowhere to remind me I'm not good enough, that I'm bad, awful…"

He just stared at her. "You know you're not. What do I need to do to convince you?"

She inhaled and lowered her gaze to his knee, seeing the dirt on his pants, and she reminded herself in that moment how lucky she was to have him. "By just reminding me, by being here, by loving me," she said.

He reached for her hand, and she took in the soft smile, the way he gave all of himself to her. At times, it still took her breath away. "You know I do," he said. "You know I would do anything for you, and you have to know that article is just their way of trying to convince themselves that they aren't evildoers. I can only imagine that it had to be easier for them to not include you, because then there would've been questions. I mean, seriously, how would it look if people learned the truth about this upscale family who are supposedly on the moral high ground, doing all this good and acting like role models? How quickly do you think their kingdom would come crashing down around them in all their hypocrisy?"

She just stared. With his smart mouth, he had a way of cutting through the bullshit and seeing people for who they really were. Yet he couldn't see his dad for who he was. "Well said," she replied. "Maybe you could keep reminding me of that, too."

"I will if you need me to. Just remember that if they showed up here, I'm not sure I would be able to forgive them for what they've done."

She just took him in, feeling that tightness in her chest. She had to remind herself to breathe.

"So you were looking for something?" he said. He

looked around as she rested her hands on his leg, his fingers taking hers, just touching her for a moment. But before long, there was a tap on the door, and she took in Todd standing there, his expression humbling before he offered her a smile.

"Sorry to interrupt you two," he said. "Andy, that guy you were waiting for to deliver the hay is here. I guess you really mean it when you say you do all the work yourself."

She just stared at Todd and the way he was playing messenger, as if he was suddenly someone of importance in Andy's life.

"Thanks, Dad. I'll be right there," Andy said, then gave her all of his attention, letting his gaze fall back on her again. "So you said it was a letter you're looking for?"

She allowed her gaze to linger on Andy and then slip over to Todd, who was still standing there in the doorway, watching her, waiting. "You know what? It's not important. I'm sure it's here somewhere. I'll find it," she said. There was something about having a wolf standing in her house, blending in with the sheep, that made her confidence and fight flicker, as if lighting a fire inside her. "I'll deal with it. I'm sure it's nothing to worry about, and if it is a problem, I'll let you know," she added, noticing as Todd held himself so still. She patted Andy's leg, and he stood up and then leaned down and pressed his lips to hers. She kissed him deeply, tasting him and letting it linger longer than she normally would've. "I love you," she said, and he smiled, his face inches from hers.

"I love you, too," he replied. Then he stepped around the desk, giving his dad a look that was all business. "Well, let's go. You wanted to help, and here's a good place to start."

She wasn't sure what to make of Todd as he stepped out, because she couldn't see his face. She wondered if he understood the fire he was playing with.

"Oh, and remember what I said," Andy called out. His hand rested on the doorframe as he jabbed his finger at the computer screen. "Leave it alone. They're not worth it, and don't punish yourself. If I could find a way to erase it from the net, you know I would."

He tapped the doorframe and left, and she watched the sexy ass of her husband stride down the hall, his father in front of him.

Todd Friessen had shown up on her doorstep and was playing games—but she could play, too, and she'd learned from the best: her husband. There was no way she was going to let Todd mess with her, with Andy, or with her children.

CHAPTER
Eleven

She pulled her light brown sweater a little tighter around herself, feeling the chill of the fall Montana night settling in as she strode to the barn and listened to the nicker of the five horses in the stalls. Pedro, Andy's paint, stuck his head over the stall door, and she ran her hand over his forelock.

"Good boy," she said, smelling the manure and fresh hay and everything that made a barn just that. It was the kind of smell people either loved or hated, which said everything about whether they would be cut out for country life. Laura loved the country, this ranch, this life, and she wouldn't have traded it for anything.

As she took in the hay stacked at the back of the barn, she still couldn't believe Todd had spent most of the day stacking it with Andy and Zac. She went up the steps, hearing the voices of Jeremy and Tiffy, and knocked at the painted white door, which was ajar.

"Hey, you two. Everyone still up?" she called as she poked her head into the open-concept two-bedroom loft, seeing Jeremy at the sink in the small kitchen, washing a frypan while Tiffy dried a cup. Her dark hair was pulled up in a high ponytail, and what looked like ketchup was spilled on her T-shirt. Jeremy had the rough look of having gone two days without shaving, and Brandon was at the small rectangular coffee table in front of the light brown sofa. The door to his bedroom was open, as was the slider to the master suite, revealing their unmade queen bed.

"Yeah, late dinner," Jeremy said. "Just cleaning up the backlog of dishes from this morning, as well. So how's it going over at the house?" He handed the frypan to Tiffy and drained the sink.

Laura stopped first at Brandon and touched the top of his head, then took in the superhero coloring book he was working on. The crayons were everywhere, and his artwork was a disaster. "Oh, that is so pretty!" she exclaimed and kissed him again on the head.

"Thanks, Grandma."

She stood up, taking in the easy chair, which held a laundry basket of clothes, and the round table with four chairs. The small island had two stools, and she strode over to where Tiffy was wiping it down, pulled out a stool, and sat.

"You didn't answer, Mom, about how everything is going over there with Gramps," Jeremy said. "Kind of got the sense from Gabriel that you aren't happy Grandfather is still here. I guess I never paid much mind to the history. You and Dad just didn't talk much about them."

Tiffy had the most amazing eyes, and the glance she gave Laura was filled with empathy, with loving support. Her lips held the hint of a smile as she rested her hands on the counter, and Laura pulled in a breath, wondering what to say. She smoothed her palm over the clean mixed green granite that Andy and Jeremy had fitted themselves.

"Not sure there are words to describe the situation," she said, "but I guess we'll start with how I can't believe he's still here. To me, the fact that your dad is letting him stay and is willing to give him the benefit of the doubt is more of a surprise than anything, considering what and who Todd Friessen is and what he's done in the past. In fact, I know he's up to something."

She flicked her gaze up to find Jeremy and Tiffy standing side by side and staring at her. She had their full attention now, and she wondered by the shocked look on their faces if they had any idea of how she was feeling. She inhaled, thankful that she was no longer being hit with the panic of not being able to breathe. It was a feeling she didn't like, one that scared her, because it was outside her control.

"So it's clear you don't like him and there's some history," Jeremy said. "I guess I just didn't realize the extent of the bad blood. I'm still trying to wrap my head around some of the things Gabriel said about him, about what he did to you, to Dad." Jeremy leaned on the counter and shrugged. "I stopped in because there was just something about the little I had heard, the way Grandfather kept referring to Gabriel with such distance. I wanted to know more, but I never could've imagined what Gabriel told me." He glanced to the side at Tiffy.

Laura could tell by that one look that they were on the same page, and evidently they both knew everything. Though Gabriel had been young, he'd been old enough to know Andy's parents hadn't wanted him. It was a horrible thing that she would likely hold against Andy's father forever, and even against his mother, who was now six feet under.

"So you know how bad it was, then," Laura said. "He hated me and still hates me because he sees both me and Gabriel as the ones who kept your father from having everything of Caroline's, from having the kind of life and power and lineage that Caroline and Todd had planned for Andy. You know, they wanted him to marry the right woman, with the right kids, because that would bring the right kind of mergers, the right deals, the right politics." She gestured vaguely and stopped to breathe. "Andy's mother was wealthy, connected, from the kind of family that really makes things happen in this country. And there was me, a nobody, as far as they were concerned."

Jeremy shook his head, shocked. Tiffy didn't seem impressed, either. Laura knew she was down to earth and grounded, and she never would've bought into that kind of life. She'd never have fit, thankfully.

"Well, do you think he's changed?" Tiffy asked, and Laura could see that it was a topic she and Jeremy had likely discussed in depth.

Maybe, she thought, but at the same time, she wondered. "He says he's changed, and your father wants to believe he has, but I know he hasn't." She actually lifted her chin, ready to stand her ground but biting her tongue about that letter.

"Then you need to tell Dad," Jeremy started. "Tell him to listen…"

There was a tap on the door, and they all turned.

"Hey, heard voices up here and thought I would come over," Todd said as he strode up into the loft. There was a moment of silence as they all stared.

"Sure, come on up," Jeremy said.

Laura pulled her gaze over to Tiffy, whose expression showed her support. Something about it said everything without words, and Laura listened to Todd's heavy footsteps, hearing only vaguely what he was saying to Brandon.

"I can color you one, too!" Brandon added joyfully.

Todd was holding the picture, staring at it as he handed it back to Brandon with a wink. "Hey, thanks. You work on that some more," he said with a smile, and she could feel her overprotective mother bear instincts, fighting the urge to move in and scoop up Brandon and get him away.

Todd's gaze met hers, and he nodded. "Laura, didn't know you were over here," he said. Wow, what was it about the way he talked to her? His disdain was there in his voice. She'd expected him to hide it better. Then he took in Tiffy and gave her a nod, as well. "Tiffy," was all he said, nothing else. Apparently she wasn't on his acceptable list, either.

He shoved his hands in the front pockets of his jeans and took a few steps around the sofa, into the dining area. "So this is the place," he said. The loft was small and cozy, an apartment that Andy had built for Jeremy. It was their space, and at the same time, it kept them there at home, where the family could be together.

"This is it. Small, cozy, but ours," Jeremy said.

Todd was nodding, and she didn't have a clue what he was thinking.

"Laura, I was going to put on the kettle," Tiffy said, then slid her gaze away. "Do you want tea, Todd?"

"None for me," Laura said.

"Was hoping for something a little stronger," Todd

said. There was no question in his deep voice, and she was stuck on how presumptuous he sounded. She felt her jaw slacken, remembering well the stocked bar of Andy's parents' estate, their nightly drinks. It was just something they had done.

"Sorry, we don't have anything stronger than apple juice," Jeremy said, then tossed an odd look her way. "So, Gramps, how long are you staying?"

The expression on Todd's face was priceless. "What is it with you young kids and your nicknames? I told you to call me Grandfather—and, honestly, I have no plans other than getting to know you kids, all my grandkids, and my great-grandson. I want to spend some time with my son, rebuilding our relationship. Andy and I were like two peas in a pod, discussing, planning, sharing. We did more business together than not. I taught him everything he knows, but he's still got some things to learn." Todd seemed to really dig in, standing his ground.

Tiffy had filled the kettle and put it on to boil, and she scraped at the ketchup on her shirt. Laura wanted to laugh. Tiffy wasn't the kind of girl to run and change just to impress someone, and she lifted her gaze to Laura. Yup, so she'd picked up on the slight to both of them and the implication of the role Todd wanted with Andy. It was unsettling.

"Oh, and what things would those be, Todd?" Laura said. She sat up straight on the stool and crossed her jean-clad legs, getting the feeling Todd was having to fight the urge to allow his gaze to drag over her the way he did with women, putting them in what she knew he saw as their place. Maybe having Jeremy standing right there, watching, was putting him on his best behavior.

"Well, business, for one, negotiations, investing, and

connecting with the kind of people who get things done," Todd said. "Andy's got a head for the kind of complicated business most folks can never figure out. He always has. Some folks belong in politics, behind the scenes, making things happen in this country, and Andy is just one of them. It comes to him naturally."

Jeremy glanced over to her, confused, and then at Tiffy, who leaned on the island. "I didn't know Dad was interested in politics?" he said.

When Laura shrugged, he dragged his gaze back to Todd, who had settled that unforgiving look on her. Then, as if he remembered himself, he pulled his gaze away and forced a smile, giving a subtle laugh that sounded so odd under his breath as he took in Jeremy with a fondness she hadn't imagined he possessed.

"He's not interested in politics, Jeremy," Laura said. "That would be your grandfather. As I recall, you and Caroline were always concerned with who Andy should be with. In fact, wasn't it a senator's daughter you were insisting he marry when he married me instead?"

She wondered if Jeremy could appear more shocked. Yes, that story was one she and Andy hadn't shared. Theirs hadn't been a love match. Instead, it had been his way of making things right for her, of rescuing her. Neither could have expected the love that had followed.

"That's water under the bridge, my dear. You know that," Todd said. "I've moved on. My son made his choice." Todd lifted his hand in the air, and Laura couldn't help herself from glancing Tiffy's way, seeing the emotion, the surprise in her expression. She didn't know what to say.

Laura had to fight the urge to roll her shoulders. She

could feel his arrogance, the way he was attempting to steamroll her and put her in her place. Yeah, she was having none of that. "I think the problem is, Todd, that you don't know your son, not really. Andy is all about family, about us. In fact, he's closer to Brad, Jed, Neil, and Rodney than he ever will be with you."

The way Todd dragged his gaze over to her had her fighting the urge to cower. It reminded her so much of staring into the eyes of a snake. "Andy is still my son, girl," he said. "Don't you forget that. When push comes to shove, he may have chosen you, chosen to settle for this—but I'm here now, and I'm going to make things right with him, because I'm his father, because I love him. I've been denied the chance to get to know my grandkids. You seem to forget your place."

She wasn't sure who was more shocked, Jeremy or Tiffy or her. Todd seemed to have forgotten for a second that he was showing a side of himself she was positive he didn't want anyone to see. Then he shook his head and lifted his hands, saying, "Sorry, that was uncalled for."

"Yeah, that's my mother you're disrespecting," Jeremy said. "This isn't just my dad's place, either. It's my mom's. Please don't ever talk to her like that again. You may be my grandfather, but that doesn't give you the right to come in here and talk to my mom the way you just did." He sounded unusually calm, but she didn't miss the edge to his voice and the warning in his words.

"Understood. I'm sorry again," Todd said to Jeremy.

"You need to apologize to my mom, not me." Jeremy lifted his hands, and she thought he was about to step back from how close Todd was to him.

"Laura, we've had our differences," Todd said, "but

I certainly didn't mean to insult you. It's just my way, and I'm doing my best to change and to make things right. It's hard for me to see the choices my son made when he had so much offered to him that most people will never have the chance for, and he tossed it away." He lifted his hand as if someone was about to interrupt. "I'm not saying this to insult you, because I can see, being here, that he's happy. I can see his love for his kids, his family. I know Andy very well, and I've never seen him so relaxed and at ease, but at the same time, I sense a restlessness in him, as if he knows he's missing something, and that is something he was born into, the kind of challenge and opportunities few can actually have."

"Todd, you're wrong," Laura said. "I think you want to find something in my husband so you can say you told him so, so you can tell him he didn't listen and that I'm the reason he had to settle for so much less. If I'm guessing correctly, isn't this really about the fact that I'm the reason you lost everything?"

He lifted his hand to brush her off, his expression very much saying that she was just an annoyance. "That's water under the bridge," he said.

"Is it? I wonder if you truly believe that." She noted he didn't look her way but instead glanced around the loft apartment. For the life of her, she wondered what he saw.

"You have no idea what it's like to have everything in your life taken away," Todd said. "Being married to Caroline was a partnership, a business arrangement, really, that worked, and it worked well, but you ruined everything. Andy never would have made the choices he made if it weren't for you."

Behind them, the floor squeaked.

"You're wrong, Dad," Andy said as he stepped up into the loft. She took in the five o'clock shadow on his face, the sleeves of his blue and white dress shirt rolled up.

Todd slid his gaze over to her before letting it land on his son. Jeremy backed away, his expression one of shock, amusement.

"I was never really happy with you," Andy said. "Then there was Caroline. With a mother like that, I'm not sure I understand how I could have any empathy at all for anyone. But after watching my wife raise our children, love them, be here with them, I've realized it's about family, Dad. What I have here is everything I never really understood I could want, because I grew up in such loveless privilege. That's the kind of life I wouldn't want for my children. Do I regret the choices I made? Of course, many."

For a second, her chest squeezed, and she had to remind herself to breathe as Andy took another step into the loft, letting his gaze linger on Brandon, who was watching and listening, and then over to Jeremy and Tiffy before finally landing on her.

"But my wife," Andy said, "my family, are not those choices." He nodded to her, and she could feel her heart ease and flow with the love she had for him. Andy took a quick breath. "No, Dad, I empathize with you and your situation and the fact that you were forced to part ways with the kind of life you expected me to have. I understand what you were grooming me for, and I understand your expectation that I would be a pawn you could use to gain money, position, power. I get it, but at the same time, Dad, you didn't exactly have the kind of lifestyle a son can be proud of. I don't want my kids knowing about it in any way—nor do I, God forbid, condone them being groomed to follow in your footsteps. The mistresses, the politicians, the backroom deals, the lying…"

Laura didn't have to look over to Jeremy to see his surprise. Tiffy had already made her way over to Brandon and slipped into the bathroom, and she could hear the bathtub running. The kettle had been turned off and sat there, steaming.

"I'm sorry that you got a shitty deal, but I'm not responsible," Andy said. "We're all responsible for ourselves. I would never put expectations on my kids about how their lives should be, because I'm centering my life, my plans, around them. I have no problem with you getting to know our kids, mine and Laura's, but at the same time, I cannot allow you to stay under this roof and not fully support my wife and respect her role here." Andy stopped talking and shook his head, determined. The way his eyes reached out to his dad, she knew there was something more, maybe from another time, from who they had once been before her.

Todd nodded. "Well, I guess maybe I should be moving on. Don't want to overstay my welcome. It was great to see you again, Andy, Jeremy." Then he took in Laura and inclined his head. She wasn't sure what it meant, but at the same time, feeling her husband pulling rank and backing her up unconditionally meant more than anything. "I'll leave tomorrow, if that's all right?"

Andy didn't say anything.

"That would be fine, Todd," Laura said and cleared her throat, then watched as he strode to the stairs. He glanced over to Andy and then her before leaving.

She listened to his footsteps and the silence in the loft, which lingered for a second.

"Well, that was interesting," Jeremy said. "So he's just going to leave, and go where?"

Andy exhaled, and she could see the heaviness wash over him as if he was considering something. Then he blinked, his expression laced with a watchful wariness she hadn't seen in a while. "I don't know where he'll go," he said, "but that's not up to us. One thing is for sure: Todd has always landed on his feet."

CHAPTER
Twelve

The water was running in the kitchen, and Andy could hear the sound of the dishwasher and the voices, the laughter, of his family. Brandon and Shaunty were running around but were quickly scooted out of the kitchen by Gabriel, who strode after them with a watchful confidence, holding the back door open as the kids laughed and jumped. His smile was all Laura, but at the same time, he was very much Andy's son. He was so damn proud of him.

"No way! I told Mom that's not how it happened," Jeremy said, laughing. Andy missed what he had said, as he couldn't see everyone in the kitchen from where he'd moved into the living room with his dad.

"Oh, you…" Laura replied and tossed a dishtowel at him.

Devon, who had pulled up earlier that afternoon, stood beside Jeremy and Zac in the kitchen and joined in the laughter that followed. All his kids were there in the heart of the home, helping Laura, Elizabeth, Tiffy, and Sara clean up and put away what was left of a burger and dog barbecue. The girls had lost the toss for the clean-up, and Andy could still picture his dad's face at the horror of their democracy.

"That's quite a brood you have, Andy," Todd said as he took in the way Gabriel wrapped his arm around Zac and gave him a noogie, that rough boy play that often went on.

Andy couldn't get over the love between his kids and the ones they loved. His family was growing, and it was in a direction that he, not his father, had set. He took in Todd, who was holding a glass of bourbon, his drink of choice. For a second, he couldn't shake a sense of pity, a feeling he'd never had for him before.

"Yeah, it is," Andy said. "This is my family, all of them."

Todd allowed his gaze to land on Gabriel and linger.

"You know," Andy continued, "out of all my kids, Gabriel is the only one you've not tried to know since being here."

His dad stilled before lifting the glass to his mouth, then seemed to change his mind as he looked at the glass and then dragged his gaze over to Andy. "He's not your son," he said.

At one time, Andy would've jumped down his dad's throat at the ignorance of the remark, but now he just shook his head. "That's where you're wrong. He is very much my son, and legally, too. I'm sorry for you that you can't see that, because it's your loss, not knowing him."

Todd made a face. Of course, he didn't get it. "You gave him your name, but he'll never really be a Friessen."

Andy could see the division clearly now. Todd Friessen was different from Rodney. He wondered how they could have grown up together yet ended up that way. All his years with Caroline and his sordid lifestyle had permanently ingrained in Todd some beliefs that Andy could see he wasn't willing to change.

"You're wrong, Dad. I'm sorry you can't see that, but understand that your kind of thinking will cost you any relationship you're thinking of having with my kids. Some of the ideas I see you still have…my kids weren't raised like that."

He wondered for a second if his dad finally got it, as his expression turned somber as he stared into his glass before lifting it and downing the last of the bourbon. When he set the glass down on the side table, he said, "Well, I guess I should be going. I have a lot of miles to cover before it gets dark."

Andy took in the black suitcase still sitting at the door. Though his father still hadn't mentioned it, he knew about the house he had in North Lakewood, small, modest. It had belonged to one of his mistresses. At least he'd had something to fall back on when he lost everything.

"So where are you going to go?" Andy said.

His father shoved his hands in the pockets of his dark dress pants. He was wearing a navy dress shirt with a classy belt, evidently still set in his ways about dressing for dinner. On a working ranch, though, dinner was all about the family coming together, not putting on a show and dressing in something they reserved only for special occasions.

"Oh, here and there," Todd said. "I have friends down in Florida, and your mother's brothers, too. We still keep in touch. One's in Boston. Maybe I can reach out to Chelsea when I'm there."

Andy didn't answer at first, just inhaled and crossed his arms over his chest, taking in his family. "Have a safe trip," he finally said. He'd talk to Chelsea and Ric, but he knew Ric would likely be more vigilant than he had been.

In the kitchen, Sara and Devon were in each other's arms, his hands on her hips, and she stood on her tiptoes and pressed a kiss to his lips before striding into the living room.

"Are you leaving, Grandfather?" she asked. Devon was behind her, and Andy could see that his dad was struggling with this match.

"Yes, Sara, my princess, I am," Todd said. "I'm going to miss you terribly." He slid his arm around Sara's shoulders, hugging her, and then started walking to the door. Yeah, Andy could see the affection his dad had for her.

"So that's your dad, huh," Devon said as he came to stand beside him.

"Yup, that's him," Andy said. What else was there to say?

"I always wondered why you are the way you are. Guess now I know," he replied.

For a second, Andy had to wonder what he meant. He dragged his gaze from Devon over to Sara and his dad, who stepped into the kitchen, where Todd was saying goodbye to everyone. When he looked back, there it was: the smirk, the smile, the teasing mischievousness that was characteristic of Devon.

"You mean handsome and brilliant?" Andy said, raising a brow.

Devon poked his side with his elbow. "No, I mean all

that uptightness. You're the only guy I ever met who could make it snow in hell."

The way Devon said it had Andy staring at the young man his daughter was head-over-heels in love with. Andy was rather fond of him. There was just something about him, but he could see so much of himself there. "Snow in hell? Not one I've heard before, but I figure I'll take it as a compliment."

Devon slapped his shoulder. His build was broad, and he was appearing more and more like a linebacker. He had strength and confidence. "Well, you do that," he teased and shook his head. His laugh always had a way of lightening the mood, and Andy listened to the laughter from the kitchen, as well. "So Sara said it's been a long time since you've seen your pops. Is this the first of many visits?"

Andy dragged his gaze back over to him from his family, who were saying goodbye to a man he couldn't believe he'd once understood. "You worried?" he said. He could give it back just as much when he wanted to.

Devon made a face and shrugged. "No, but would be nice to have a heads-up if it's going to become, like, a regular thing and all…"

"It's not." Andy cut him off. "Todd's Todd, you know. When you're a kid, you can't pick who your family is, but when you're an adult, this amazing thing happens and you suddenly get to decide who you want in your life. My dad's views on you being black and Sara being white come from the same place as his issues with me and Laura. That's one of the reasons he isn't in my life, our lives."

"Who's black? Jeremy asked as he strode in, holding a beer, with a two-day beard on his face and mustard on his long-sleeved white and blue jersey. He looked from Devon to Andy, realizing he'd walked in on the middle of a conversation.

"Me, apparently. Your gramps has issues," Devon said.

The expression on Jeremy's face was priceless as he dragged his gaze from Andy to Devon. "Oh, well, glad you pointed that out. So are we still on for Thursday, the game? I'll pick you up, and Sara and Tiffy can do the sisterly hangout thing, dinner and a movie, while I get my guy bonding time…"

Andy shook his head and walked away as Devon and Jeremy made their plans, the basketball game. He was glad at how close they'd become.

Todd lifted his hand in a wave as he stepped out of the kitchen, then rested his hand on his shoulder. They were still the same height, and Andy could see the arrogance that made up who his dad was. "Andy, it was great seeing you, son," he said.

"Have a safe trip. I'll walk you out," he replied, then lifted the suitcase and strode down to the BMW parked out front. His dad opened the trunk, and he lifted the suitcase in. As he closed the trunk and took in the house, he could feel the energy of his family inside. "You know," he said, "my wife owes you nothing."

For a minute, Todd had the strangest look on his face. Yeah, that letter he'd found in the mail at the back door, addressed to his wife, was now tucked in the file where he kept their taxes, because he knew that was the one place Laura wouldn't look. The second he'd seen it, he just hadn't been able to shake the feeling that it was something his dad would do.

"So you've made clear," Todd said. "Never would

have picked this for you, Andy, my boy. For my brother's kids, yeah, but I always wanted more for you. I guess it's really water under the bridge, isn't it? Your kids are grown, you have a grandson, and you really are willing to settle for a simple life, a life that has no meaning."

The way Todd said it, Andy still wondered how he could have turned out as well as he did. He glanced up to the house, seeing Laura step out with Jeremy, Gabriel, and Elizabeth as Shaunty and Brandon ran up the steps.

"If being happy means a simple life, then yeah, I have more than I ever expected to have," Andy replied. "My life may not be what you wanted for me, but it's so much better than I could ever have planned for. And as far as the letter goes, the one you sent to my wife…" He took in the way his dad's brow furrowed, the way his expression changed to confusion.

"What letter?" He shrugged, holding his car keys.

"You didn't send a letter addressed to my wife, saying, 'You owe me'?" Andy asked.

This time, Todd gave him an odd smile as he patted his shoulder and walked around to the driver's side, where he pulled open the door. "Not me, Andy," he said, then gestured with his chin to the house, where he knew Laura was on the front porch, watching. "Maybe someone else has it in for that wifey of yours. Can't help you there. Women, you know," was all he said before he slid behind the wheel, started the BMW, wheeled it around, and drove away.

Andy stared for a moment at the dust before he started back to the house and up the steps to his wife, who was now alone on the porch. She slid her arm around his waist, and his arm went instinctively around her as she leaned into him.

"You okay that he's gone?" she asked, and he wasn't sure what emotion was in her voice.

"Yeah. Don't think we'll be seeing him again," he added, and she seemed to relax. "But thanks, in case I didn't say it, for humoring me. Maybe it was because of Cancun and what almost happened."

Laura didn't say anything for a second. "Hmm, I get it, Andy. I do."

He leaned down and kissed her lips, then pulled back. "You know, with everything, I didn't get a chance to talk to you about that letter."

Her eyes widened, and she stepped back. He could see the emotion in her face. "The one that said, 'You owe me'?"

"Yeah, that very same one," he said. "I found it the night my dad showed up, and I thought it was him."

Laura's expression said everything.

"But it wasn't," he finally said.

Her jaw slackened, and she turned and stared out at the dust in the distance from Todd's car. "Are you sure?"

He looked down at Laura and then into the house. "Pretty sure. I called him out just now. Didn't seem to know anything about the letter or sending it. How did it come, anyway? I didn't see a postmark."

She pursed her lips. "Courier. Sara was there. I had to sign for it. So if it wasn't Todd, then who could it be?"

He inhaled. His chest was tight with an unsettled feeling he hadn't felt in a long time. "I don't know," he said. He lifted his arm, and Laura walked into it.

"Should I worry that someone else has it in for me, or do you think this is just some game or someone's weird, sick sense of humor?" she said.

He took in the road. He couldn't see his dad's car anymore, just the skyline, the countryside, and no one else. "No, don't worry. If it's someone just messing around, they'll soon find out they've picked the wrong man's wife to mess with."

Laura slipped both her arms around him and hugged him, pressing her chin into his chest as she looked up. She smiled. He loved her smile. "Well, Mister Friessen, you just know all the right things to say to a girl," she said and laughed, and he slid his hands over her cheeks, taking in the joy in her green eyes.

"You know it," he said, "but you know what else? I have a lot more really interesting, deeply personal, private things to say to my girl. So how about we kick the kids out of the house and retire to our room, and I show you instead of tell you?"

Her laugh was soft and teasing. "Well, that definitely sounds like a conversation I want to have." She rose up on her tiptoes, and he leaned in and kissed her again. She pulled away and pulled open the screen door, then glanced back to him. "Oh, and you get the honors of sending the kids on their way while I go run the bath."

He laughed. A few seconds later, he heard her in the house, and his kids, and he found himself glancing out into the distance again, wondering if there was always going to be someone who wanted something from him, his wife, his family.

He kicked at a clump of dirt on the porch, took in all the cars, and listened to the laughter inside. He really did have everything he'd never thought he wanted—and that letter was just another reason why Andy Friessen kept his family close.

Unfinished Business

L aura thought she should treat herself, considering the last few days. She now lingered in a nightshirt, her housecoat pulled on overtop, holding a coffee as she lounged in the easy chair in the living room. She was just up from bed, and she wasn't in any hurry to get dressed. This would be a day for her to just breathe.

The relief she felt was not lost on her. The feeling of drowning and not being able to breathe had plagued her during Todd's visit, likely from having to face a past she'd thought she had made peace with. Evidently not.

There was something about having a lack of control over her world, her family, her life, that made her worry she might lose what she had. The outside was threatening her peaceful, comfortable world and turning it upside down, and there was no rational explanation, either, for why this was happening at this point in her life.

At least Todd was now gone, and she hoped he'd never come back. At the same time, she was also glad for the chance to face him, because she wasn't that same terrified young woman she once had been, and he would never hold any power over her again.

Then there was that letter, which she was positive had come from Todd. She was still having troubling believing he wouldn't do such a thing. It had left her with a big question mark about who could be behind it. She knew Andy now had the letter and would likely be doing everything he could to find out who had sent it.

His obsessive need to protect all of them infuriated her at times, but it had given her this peace, this imperfect life that was absolutely perfect.

She lifted her mug and downed the rest of her coffee, then leaned her head back and shut her eyes, enjoying the moment as she listened to the sound of a vehicle approaching. It took another second before her eyes flew open at the unfamiliarity of it, and she stood up so fast that she stubbed her toe on the leg of the coffee table.

"Shit!" She hopped and then hobbled to the window, holding the empty mug. A black sedan she didn't recognize pulled up, and only Tiffy's car and Andy's truck were parked outside beside it. Evidently, Jeremy was gone, and Sara and Zac were as well. School was back in session today, and everyone's life was continuing.

The only thing she could think of was that her peaceful, tranquil morning was being interrupted yet again. Like, what the hell? They lived in the middle of nowhere, yet people felt they could just show up.

She rested her hand on the V neck of her silky housecoat, which stopped at midthigh. She was barefoot, her legs bare too. From the vehicle emerged a woman and a man, neat but casual, middle aged, one with salt and pepper hair, the other with a short light bob.

She ran to dress quickly, unable to help feeling pissed over these constant interruptions to her morning. Once back at the screen door, she glanced over to the barn, hoping Andy was around, but she didn't see him. Evidently, he was out somewhere and hadn't seen the car pull in, or she knew without a doubt he'd have been there to find out who the hell they were.

"Are you lost?" Laura called out, but then, they appeared too official. The man wore a wrinkled white dress shirt, sleeves rolled up, with glasses, and the woman wore the same version with a jacket over her arm.

"Hope not," she replied. "Is this the Friessen residence?" She had no twang to her voice, so Laura figured she wasn't from around there.

"It is, and you are…?" She let the question linger as she stepped outside, the screen door slapping closed behind her. She wasn't too inclined to invite strangers in, considering the pattern of uninvited guests they'd had that week.

"Oh, sorry about that," the woman replied. "The name's Fran Ostley, and this is my colleague, Ray Cooper. We're with the *Post*, out of Washington." Fran was now on the steps, holding a portfolio briefcase under her arm, and she held out her hand. "I can see by your expression that we're likely not who you expected."

Laura shook her hand, taking in the man as well, who was looking around with an odd expression, checking things out, investigating—prying, nosy, and something else.

"The *Post*?" Laura asked, feeling uneasy, and she took in the way the two glanced to each other.

"Sorry, the *Christian Post*, the largest Christian news source," Ray said, then reached up and extended his hand. "And you are?"

"Laura," was all she said, feeling very much intruded upon. Why was it that it seemed they'd just hit the jackpot, by the expression on their faces?

"Laura Friessen, formerly Parnell?" Ray said.

It was instinctive, the way her jaw clamped down, and she felt herself grinding her teeth. Like, what the fuck! "Yes, I'm Laura Friessen. Parnell is my maiden name. So what can I do for you?"

She glanced out to the barn, looking for signs of life from anyone, Tiffy, Andy. Where the hell were they?

"We're actually covering a story about George and Sue Parnell," said Fran. "They've been the biggest benefactors of a school in Africa, and with all the good works they've done, along with their two sons, Brian and Chad…"

So these two were reporters, but why were they there? Evidently, the craziness was going to continue in her life. She forced herself to pull in a breath when it hit her, the flutter of panic, but when she lifted her gaze to the barn again, she saw Tiffy hurrying her way, pulling on a shoe as she ran. Her hair was hiked up in a messy bun, and she wore a bulky sweater over what looked like baggy PJ pants. It was a sight, and Laura felt her jaw slacken. At the same time, she felt the support.

"I'm coming…!" Tiffy called, jogging and stumbling. For a minute, both Fran and Ray seemed to stare in shock, while Laura was fighting the urge not to laugh. "Sorry, I didn't hear the car pull up. I went back to sleep after Jeremy took Brandon to preschool on his way to work. I have the day off, and the only thing I wanted to do was sleep in another hour or two…"

Tiffy jogged up the stairs, looking as if she really had jumped right from bed. She gestured to Fran and Ray, who were still staring at her as if she'd lost her mind, and Laura knew she could introduce her to them, but she chose not to.

"Apparently, Fran and Ray here are from the *Post*," she said, "a newspaper in Washington?"

"Actually, we're digital now, but yes, we're from Washington. And you are?" Fran said. It seemed Ray was more interested in looking around, and he pulled out his phone and held it up to take their photo.

"Hey, excuse me! Don't do that," Laura snapped. "I do not want my photo taken. For the love of God, we're in our pajamas. You show up here ridiculously early, with not even a phone call, and I'm still trying to understand what it is you want with me." She felt Tiffy's hand on her arm and glanced her way.

"Well, we're trying to find out your relationship with the Parnells," Ray said. "They've been noticed by the president for all their humanitarian work, and they're up for a presidential medal of freedom. When that happens, backgrounds get checked. The recent interview in *Christian New Beginning* seems to have missed a daughter, Laura, which our team flagged. I presume that's you?" He was still holding his phone up, and she wondered if he'd snap another photo.

"Who are the Parnells, your parents?" Tiffy whispered to her, wide eyed. Laura glanced her way, feeling her hand slide around her elbow as she bumped against her. She just shook her head, still annoyed.

"I think I asked you to stop with the photos," Laura said. "Please put down your phone. You know what? This is completely inappropriate, and I'm not comfortable answering your questions. A presidential award? Well, good for them, but that's got nothing to do with me, so I'm going to ask you to leave."

"What's going on here?" Andy called out, coming around the side of the house on horseback. He took in Fran and Ray, then her and Tiffy.

"Oh, I called Andy as soon as I saw them," Tiffy whispered and nudged Laura, who wondered whether the reporters had heard.

"They're reporters from some Christian online news source," Laura said as Andy climbed out of the saddle, grabbed the reins of the paint, and walked it over to the rail of the house. He ran his hand over the backside of the horse and then pulled off his leather gloves and slapped them against his hand.

"And why are you here?" he said, not really a question but a demand. "Laura, why don't you and Tiffy go inside?"

For a second, she was about to say no, but she realized how she was dressed. It felt awkward, and here was her moment to escape.

"Just a moment before you go, Laura," Fran said. "Can you tell us why your parents omitted you from the article and never mentioned having a daughter?"

She took in the way Andy's gaze darkened. Evidently, Fran wasn't intimidated by tall, dark, and dangerous husbands like Andy. Laura pressed her lips together, because this was ridiculous and personal and not their damn business.

"Laura…" Andy said. She knew he wanted her to

go inside, and she felt Tiffy's hand on her arm as she heard the door squeak. She gave Andy a nod and turned, starting in after Tiffy.

"Laura," Fran continued, "do you have any comment on the rumors that your brother was found together with a man, or your parents' statement that those rumors are false?"

She stilled, her back to the reporters, and took in the shock on Tiffy's face. When she turned around, Andy was shaking his head. "Gay…I'm sorry, who?" she asked.

Fran opened her portfolio and pulled out a paper. "Ah, Chad Parnell, married to Donna, with two daughters. His wife has recently filed for divorce, and our news department has just learned of a drunken statement where he's been quoted as saying he's gay."

Well, that was news to her. She pulled in a breath and took in Andy as he strode up the steps and around Fran until he was standing right in front of her, his back to Laura. She stepped inside and let the screen door close.

"My wife has no comment, so I'd like you to leave," Andy said. "This really has nothing to do with us."

She couldn't make out what else he was saying as she turned into the house and took in Tiffy, whose expression was one of shock.

"Well, there really is never a dull moment around here," Tiffy said.

Laura strode into the kitchen just as she heard car doors, then a car starting, and then Andy stepped inside, holding a business card. "So you chased them away."

He nodded. "For now."

"I came over as soon as I saw them," Tiffy said. "I

heard what you said to Jeremy about strangers and people showing up here."

Andy just nodded, and Laura felt very much in the dark.

"So let me get this straight: You told Jeremy to do what, exactly?" she said.

"To watch the house," Andy said. "If anyone comes lurking, I want him to be over here if I'm not around."

Tiffy shrugged. "So what's the issue? I'm not sure I'm understanding what they wanted, exactly."

"Evidently, my parents don't have the perfect family, after all, or the perfect image," Laura said. "I'd say they came looking for dirt."

"Hmm," was all Andy said, wearing an odd expression. Laura could always tell when he was considering something.

"And that would be?" Tiffy still wore a look that was all confusion.

"Well, I would have said the dirt was me, except apparently there's something worse than kicking out a daughter who got pregnant at fifteen," Laura said. "By the sounds of those reporters out there, it seems having a gay son definitely tops the list."

Andy watched as Laura, who'd grabbed a quick shower, dressed in a pair of blue jeans and a light T-shirt. Her wavy blond hair was brushed and hanging damp past her shoulders as she paced the living room with the phone to her ear, calling her brother from the numbers he'd stored on his phone.

"So Laura hasn't seen her family in years," said Tiffy, "and then there was your dad, who showed up here out of the blue. A presidential award is pretty spectacular, but I can tell by your face that you're not happy about any of this. Andy, what are you worried about?" Tiffy had a way of talking and trying to make sense of a situation that was both amusing and endearing. He tried not to laugh, knowing Tiffy would be on board with whatever they decided. It was never a question. They were a family—she got that.

"Well, I left a message with Brian this time," Laura said. "The number you have for Chad is no longer in service. Should I call my parents? Not that they'd want to talk to me, but seriously, this feels like shit hitting the fan, like I'm being dragged into something I'm not really understanding, nor do I want to know anything about it. Do you really think Chad is gay? That would be like a nail in my parents' coffin, the kind of imperfection they can't have. I mean, look at me. I'm apparently the black sheep who goes without a mention, but Chad…well, that would be scandalous to them. Would love to know if it's true." Laura furrowed her brow. This was the first time Andy had heard her talk about her family without it seeming as if she was still carrying that world of hurt.

"Does it matter?" Tiffy said. She still needed to brush her hair and was staring at Laura and then Andy, questioning as if waiting for a clue on how she was supposed to be backing them up.

"Nope," Laura said, "but if my brother is gay, and this is how it came out, then I can just imagine the horror my parents would be feeling right now. Gay is gay, as long as it's not their son."

Tiffy's mouth was a big O as if she got it, but then her expression became confused again. "So you're telling me that being gay is, like…I'm sorry, I guess you lost me on how being gay is a problem."

"It's not, Tiffy," Laura said. "The problem is George and Sue Parnell and their need for a perfect family image. Being up for a presidential freedom award is a very big deal, but having a scandal would be a disaster in their eyes." She lifted her hands.

Andy just watched as she rinsed out the coffee pot and set it back in the coffeemaker, then started running water in the sink as if getting ready to clean up.

"What did you say to the reporters to make them leave?" Tiffy said, turning to Andy. "And why were they here, anyway? Give them the damn award if they want, but why track you down? I don't understand."

Andy took in Laura, who rolled her shoulders and tilted her head from side to side. He could see she was trying to work out the tension, so he stepped up behind her, rested his hands on her shoulders, and rubbed, massaging the tightness.

"Oh, that feels good. You're hired," she groaned.

He leaned down and couldn't resist kissing her forehead as she leaned back. "Well, that's what reporters do," he said. "Someone obviously stumbled on something, and now they want the dirt…"

The phone rang, and they all stared at it, but Andy grabbed it before Laura could see the name on the screen: B. Parnell.

"Hello?" Andy said, feeling Laura's hand on his arm, pulling at him. Of course, she wanted the phone.

"Hey, this is Brian Parnell. Is this Andy, Laura's husband?" It was a deep voice, unrecognizable.

"Yeah, this is Andy Friessen. Thanks for calling back, Brian. Laura was actually trying to call your brother, Chad, but the numbers I have for you both are pretty old. Chad's was disconnected." He took in the way Laura gestured with her hand. Of course she wanted to talk. "Hey, Brian, Laura's right here and wants to talk. I'm going to put you on speakerphone." He pressed the button and put the phone back in the holder.

"Hi, Brian, this is Laura," she said.

"Hey, Laura, great to hear from you. It's been how many years?"

Andy wasn't sure what to make of the expression on

Laura's face as she said, "Twenty-something, a long time."

"Yeah, sorry, I should have reached out to you. It's life, you know, got in the way."

Laura nodded. Andy had never understood why her brothers never reached out. He'd given them his contact information and had expected to hear from them at some point. It was disappointing.

"Yeah, listen, Brian," Andy said. "We were paid a visit today by two reporters about that article about your parents and you and Chad and all the work they've done in Africa. It seems the medal your parents are up for has people doing some digging, and they found out about Laura, whom the article didn't mention. But that's not all they were asking."

Laura stood with her arms crossed.

Tiffy was behind them, leaning on the island, listening intently. "Hey," she said. "I feel kind of like a third wheel here, so I thought I should introduce myself. I'm Tiffy, Andy and Laura's daughter-in-law, who's married to Jeremy, their son—and you have no idea who I am." Her expression was priceless as she made a face to Andy. He just shook his head.

"Ah, okay…nice to meet you through the phone. So this is kind of weird," Brian said.

Tiffy held up her hands in surrender. "Hey, I'll say, but I thought the only polite thing would be to say hi and let you know I'm listening in."

Andy didn't miss the tug at the sides of Laura's lips as she tried not to smile. He too couldn't help lifting a brow as he tossed Tiffy an amused glance over his shoulder. She shrugged. She fit just perfectly into their family.

"Yeah…" was all Brian said.

"So, Brian, the reporters," Laura said. "I don't owe Mom and Dad anything, but I'm not sure what's going on with Chad…"

Brian sighed into the phone. "Look, Laura, I felt really bad about that article and how it came out. You should know your name never came up. It wasn't that Mom and Dad were purposely trying to say they didn't have a daughter—it was just about us and the work they did, and the work Chad and I did in the background to help them. The reporter who did the article assumed there were no other children. I told them when we saw the final article that they needed to say something, but they didn't. I'm sorry about that, but you know how Mom is."

Andy didn't miss the shadow that seemed to cast over Laura. It was there in her frown, in the way she shrugged as if she was struggling not to give them a pass and say something ridiculous like *Yeah, that's okay.*

"Regardless, it was a shitty thing to do, just one more slap to my wife," Andy said. "I didn't appreciate it, Brian—and it isn't just them. You could have said something, too."

Laura pulled in a breath as if thinking, then slid her gaze over to him. He could see hurt, remorse, and a lot of emotion. Then she shook her head.

"Okay, I hear you," Brian said. "In hindsight, yeah, but at the same time, this article wasn't about Laura. I'm sorry, Laura, but it was about Mom and Dad and the work they're doing, and Chad and I…" Brian sighed. "Yeah, then there's Chad. Were they asking about him?"

At the way Brian asked, Laura slid her gaze over to him. She'd picked up on it, too. "Of course they were, Brian," she said. "They asked me about Chad being gay, about him being married, too, with kids. So, like, what is that about?" Laura gestured at the phone as if Brian was right there.

The silence lingered for a second, and then there was tapping in the background. Brian pulled in a breath. "Well, the thing is that I'm not really comfortable talking about this. Chad is kind of a disappointment right now. He's had some issues."

"What…what issues? Come on. For fuck's sake, Brian, it's a simple question. Is Chad gay? Not that it's an issue." Laura was shaking her head.

"He says he is, but we're thinking it's just a phase, as he and Donna have had a rough patch. There's a friend who's been around, and he's leaned on him way too much. He's just strayed, is all. He'll get his head together. He'll get his family back together."

Andy didn't miss the way Laura stilled. He was having a hard time wrapping his head around what Brian was saying, as if Chad was just having some fun or was confused. This was crazy.

"It doesn't work that way, Brian," Andy said. "If he's gay, it's not a lifestyle choice. It's who he is."

"Look, you don't know the situation," Brian said. "Donna and Chad are married and have been together a lot of years. They have two teenage daughters. He's not gay. I don't care what he's saying or what the reporters are saying. He can't be, because then his entire marriage would be a lie, and could you imagine how Donna would feel? This is killing her now, and their daughters. If the reporters come back, just tell them that they're misinformed, that Chad was going through a rough time, but he's got his head screwed back on straight. We've made sure of it."

Andy had to pull his hand over his face as he listened. "Look, Brian, I guess you're not hearing me," he said. "I don't want my wife involved in this, nor do I want reporters showing up here. We're not going to start spouting off the party line you want people to believe. We're not getting involved."

"Fine, then don't talk to them," Brian said. "This is about Mom and Dad being recognized by the president. The medal of freedom is such an incredible honor to be given, and this kind of smear campaign right before-hand isn't okay."

"It's not a smear campaign if it's true, Brian. It's just the truth coming out," Laura cut in. "So where is Chad?" Her arms were crossed, and she was determined.

"He's away," Brian said. "I made him take some time up at the family cabin, you know, at the lake. Told him to get his head screwed on straight. Look, Laura, I'm sorry you got dragged into this. Everything that happened was a long time ago. Do Mom and Dad have regrets? Sure, but at the same time, they shouldn't be crucified for something that happened years ago. None of that should take away from all the good they're doing now."

Laura pressed her hands to her face and then pulled them away. She looked tired, fed up.

"It's great to hear from you, though," Brian said. "It really has been too long. We should make time to catch up someday."

The way he said it, Andy knew he never had any intention of reconnecting with his sister. It was sad, a shame, but at the same time, he didn't want them in her life.

"Sure, someday," was all Laura said. Then she ended the call before Brian could say anything else and walked out of the kitchen.

Andy took in the shock, the odd expression on Tiffy's face as she said, "So should I stay, talk to Laura, man the door…?"

He just shook his head. "No, enjoy your day off," he said. "But hey, Tiffy…" he called out as she started out of the kitchen. She turned in the doorway, and he took in her baggy outfit, realizing she had come running without a second thought. "Thanks for having Laura's back."

She just shrugged. "Well, of course I do," she said, then started out the door and down the steps, and Andy couldn't shake the image of her like an untrained gangly pit bull at the door.

Fifteen

"Where are you going?" Andy said.

Laura had pulled out an overnight bag and was stuffing in jeans, underwear, and socks, then rummaging in her shirt drawer for a T-shirt and pajamas. What else?

She turned and took in Andy, how he stood in their bedroom, his hands on his hips, looking down at her. Of course, he looked irritated. This whole mess that had landed on her doorstep, their doorstep, had made her realize she had so much unfinished business.

She pulled in a breath and rested her hand on the dresser. "I'm going to see Chad. He's staying up at the lake."

Andy wasn't necessarily an expressive man, but he looked at her now as if he couldn't believe what she was saying and shook his head. "No, you're not. Stay out of it. This has nothing to do with you…"

"No, Andy, it has everything to do with me," she said, nearly cutting him off.

He pulled his hand over his face. Yeah, she knew

how to push his buttons. He turned around and shut the bedroom door even though there was no one else in the house. His hand was still on the knob when he turned to her and really looked at her. She could see he was thinking, likely ready to tell her no again. He was bossy, demanding, and as she waited, she realized he didn't understand how she was feeling.

She went around the bed and sat on his side, facing him. "Look, this week has been the most unusual week of surprises, and it seems it's not over. I'm wondering now what else is coming. At the same time, so much feels unfinished for me…"

He went to interrupt, but she lifted the flat of her hand and then reached over and touched his before pulling back.

"No, hear me out, Andy," she said. "You've really kept me safe, all of us. Moving us out here, it's like we've been living in a cocoon. I've felt safe and protected and comfortable, and when that letter arrived, when your dad showed up and that article came out about my parents, with no mention of me, I seriously felt as if the rug had been pulled out from under me. My quiet existence here with you, with the kids, was completely disrupted. Now I'm feeling as if I'll never have that untouched peace again, and I've realized, Andy, that I've never really closed the door on most of my past."

She could see the confusion, as if he didn't understand. Then there was amusement as he leaned against the door and he crossed his arms, staring down at her. "I don't understand where you think there's something unfinished…" he started, and she pulled in another breath, the sound of her frustration. "Fine, I'm listening," he said.

Well, that was a first, and a start. "Good, well, you know you have a way of handling everything, like you're doing right now. When your dad treated me like absolute crap—"

"He's gone. I took care of it," he said. There he went, cutting her off again.

She sighed, reminding herself to breathe. He just couldn't let her handle anything. He'd always had that controlling side of him, wanting to fix everything as if he were the only one who could do it. She loved him for it, but at the same time, it could be ridiculously exasperating.

"You're not getting it," she said through gritted teeth. "And you're not letting me talk."

This time, by the way he pulled in a breath, it sounded as if he were the one who was frustrated. She knew he didn't like to reason with her, especially when it came to them and his need to protect all of them. It was about a loss of control, and Andy didn't like feeling that way when it came to anything about his family.

"Then explain it to me," he said.

She lifted a brow. He must have got it, as he lifted his hands and said nothing else, so she began: "Yes, you asked your dad to go, but having him here and feeling that really creepy feeling, knowing he thought I was beneath him and worthless, someone of no importance, I remembered how it felt to have no voice. I mean, Andy, you swooped in and married me to protect me and Gabriel, then moved us out here with the twins to get us away from your family.

"Then there are my parents. When Gabriel had leukemia, we went there and begged and pleaded for help, and we got it from Brian, but I never got any closure on my past. Your dad, my parents…and then there's that letter. You said it wasn't your dad, so someone else out there apparently has an axe to grind with me. I have no idea for what, but at the same time, standing up to your dad, standing my ground here, was my way of taking back some of the power he's always had over me. And with my parents, it's the same thing. We cut ties, we have nothing to do with each other, because I'm their big disappointment…"

She had to lift a hand when he went to interrupt again. "Look, Andy, let me finish. I know you don't like to talk about your feelings, and when you hear me say I feel like I'm powerless or less than, you always tell me to stop it, not to think like that. You seem to think that's all it's going to take, but it doesn't work that way. I feel, I think, I still carry shame even though, logically, it's ridiculous. I know that, but that's just how my parents made me feel, as if I was nothing and worthless, as if their image is more important than me. Wow, I've never said that before. Their image is more important than their children. Even Brian appears to have fallen into line, based on what I could tell from our conversation this morning."

Andy was still leaning against the door, considering. She knew he was taking the time to really listen to her. "It happens, you know," he said. "He's under your parents' influence, so he's now acting as they want. Not surprising, Laura, considering he's never once, in all these years, reached out to you and tried to reconnect. He may have been only seventeen when he donated to Gabriel, when I left him with our phone number, our contact information, but not once has he or Chad called in the years since. Your mom and dad, on the other hand, I never expected to hear from them. I wondered how they couldn't apologize and beg your forgiveness, but your mom is a hard woman, unwilling to admit she's wrong, and your dad, as soon as I met him, I realized he's the kind of guy who falls in line with his wife's thinking."

The way he said it, she had to stifle the urge to smile, because she knew well what he thought of her parents. Andy would be the last man standing to ever go along with a woman just because she expected him to. He was too strong minded, strong willed, someone who lived and died by what he believed—but at least he was hearing her.

"Yes, and you're right," Laura replied, "but standing up to your dad was a huge coup for me. Now, understanding the kind of man he is, I'm not powerless anymore. It's like I've checked off something that's been left undone for so long. But my parents, my family, and Chad and the shitstorm of controversy and dirt and scandal that landed here at our door…well, I'm sorry, but I need to go talk to him. I don't know what will come of it, but if he's in trouble…" She wanted—no, needed to talk to him, because she understood better than anyone what was acceptable and not for her parents.

"It's not your business, Laura, not anymore," Andy said.

She knew what he meant, but she shook her head. "You're wrong, Andy. It is. I was a young, impressionable, confused teen, vulnerable and alone, when my parents kicked me out because of bad choices I made. Instead of helping me and forgiving me, they made me feel as if what I had done was the worst thing ever, and that hurt. That doubt crushed me and my confidence for so long, Andy. I realized when I saw that article and when the reporters showed up here, knocking on the door, that I still feel some embarrassment over it, as if I have to deny my existence to and for them. I'm not having that anymore. If Chad is gay, so be it. That's who he is. If he's not…" She shook her head.

She could see she'd somehow managed to get through to Andy. It was there in the love, the understanding in his eyes, which he couldn't hide, not from her.

"Well, what are you going to do? It's not your battle," he added.

She lifted her hands and then let them fall. He was right, and she knew what he was saying should make sense. "I know, but at the same time, I feel unless I resolve everything, all these little things from what feels like another lifetime, this week is going to keep happening over and over. I need to take back my power, this piece of me that everyone still has," she said. "You know what? Nothing may happen with Chad, with my mom and dad, but I need to at least be the one who buries these skeletons once and for all. I don't know what will come of it, but I do know that I don't want one more person, one more thing, knocking on our door and making me feel insignificant."

Andy said nothing, and she wasn't sure what he was thinking as he glanced over to the window, then pushed away from the door. "Fine, so you're leaving now, and it can't wait?"

She pushed off the bed and stood up, took another step, and closed the gap between them. She rested her hands on his arms and touched him so gently, feeling his strength, his passion, and everything she loved about him. She lifted her gaze, shook her head. "Nope, because waiting becomes overthinking and then chickening out, and I'm done being scared and hiding and feeling as if so much has been left unsaid. I'm leaving as soon as I pack a bag and load it in the SUV."

Andy lifted his hand and touched her chin, the side of her face, her hair. "And for how long are you planning to be gone?"

Wow, this was easier than she'd thought. "Overnight. I should be there in a few hours. I'll grab a hotel in town and then be back later tomorrow." Though, she thought, that would depend on what happened.

"Great," Andy replied. "Give me an hour to talk to Jeremy and Gabriel. They can handle things here with Zac and Sara."

"What? Wait…you're coming too?"

His hand slid under her chin, and she took in that wolfish smile. He still had the ability to shock the shit out of her. Why hadn't she expected this? "You think I'm letting you walk into this alone? As you said, problems have been crawling out of the woodwork all week. Nah, I think not. Finish packing, and I'll take our things to the car. But hear me, Laura: As far as Chad is concerned, whatever mess he's involved in, it's not up to you to fix it, and I'm sure in the hell not letting him drag you into anything."

Then he leaned in slowly and kissed her. Her head was reeling as she felt his lips on hers, soft, tender, possessive, and then he pulled back. Although Andy had listened to her, there wasn't a chance she was going to convince him to let her go alone.

CHAPTER
Sixteen

ad Laura really thought he'd let her walk out of the house with just a bag and drive away, leaving him there wondering what the hell she was walking into? Her family was a hot mess, and their shit had landed on their doorstep, considering the reporters. Though he'd sent them on their way, telling them there was no story and if they printed anything about his wife, they'd be dealing with his lawyers, had they heeded him and heard his threat? He didn't know.

He knew wariness, knew the moment someone realized he wasn't the kind of man to let anyone just walk in and threaten his family. He sure as shit wasn't going to let Laura face her family alone, not when they hadn't had the decency to reach out after all these years and at least apologize for how they had treated her.

Then there was Laura, seated beside him in his pickup. She had said only a few words since they'd left on their drive to Sandpoint, where her parents had owned a cottage on the lake since she was a kid.

"Andy, I know you have trouble with things outside your control," she said. He listened to the rustle, feeling her gaze on him, and he glanced over from the road. His wife wore dark shades that reflected the sign showing the miles that led to Sandpoint. They'd covered a lot of ground, but there was something uneasy about the distance falling away.

"That's not true," he said. "There are lots of things outside my control." He didn't miss the tug of her lips, the amusement she didn't try to hide, or the rude sound she made.

"Yeah, you're so full of shit," she said. "Case in point, Andy, my love, is that you're sitting behind the wheel with me parked in the passenger seat, insisting on coming with me to stand in the background while I speak with my brother…" She slid her sunglasses down, and he glanced over to see her gorgeous green eyes, the mischief. She was letting him know that she was the one humoring him. There was something about her standing up for herself that he was having trouble with, but at the same time, there wasn't a chance in hell he would ever admit that to her. "And I will have you know, what I have to say is coming from me, not you," she said. "So I need you to promise me you won't interrupt, no matter what. You don't always have to protect me."

He felt his fingers curl around the steering wheel. Did she have any idea how wrong she was?

"Turn right at the next roundabout," she said. "Wow, I can't believe how things haven't changed here." She was looking out the passenger window.

Sometimes it felt as if they'd been together a lifetime. He just couldn't remember with clarity his life before, being selfish, lonely, and cold, not who he was now.

"You're wrong," he said. "I do have to protect you. I'm not promising that." He knew he sounded arrogant.

"Andy…"

"No, listen, Laura. There's no way in hell I'm letting you near anyone who thinks they can treat you like dirt or say or do anything to hurt you. You seem to forget, all these years we've been together, when I moved us away from my family and kept you and our kids cocooned, as you said…that's who I am. I'm not changing, and I'm not comfortable with you thinking that you need to face these people. They're not your family. I'm your family. They're just the misfortune you had to go through as a child. I love you, but don't ask me to stand by and let anyone say anything to you that could hurt you, because I won't do that. I'd just as soon turn this truck around and take you home and have you be furious with me, because at least you'd be safe." He could feel his heart pound.

She gestured to the roundabout again, and he took the turn, spotting Sandpoint in the distance. "Andy, I won't break. I'm a lot stronger than you think I am." She sounded so reasonable, and when she spoke that calmly, there were times he just couldn't say no to her.

He exhaled and took in the signs ahead, the roads and the traffic beyond the red light at the outskirts of town. He pulled up and stopped, then took in his wife, who was watching him. He could see her patience, but then, she had to deal with the likes of him. "I know you are, Laura, but I'm not strong enough to stand by and watch anyone hurt you. I remember how haunted you were. I've seen you at your lowest, and I'm not strong enough to just sit back and let you walk into danger alone. I'm sorry if that sounds selfish, but if something is within my control, if I can prevent you from being hurt or put in danger, then I will. I'll make sure you're safe, and the kids, because I sure as shit don't plan on being in this life without you."

He wasn't sure what to make of the shock on her face, the way her mouth gaped, the breath that escaped.

"Well, okay then," she said. "But you realize that going to see Chad isn't putting my life in danger."

He knew she was right, but at the same time, no one was as predictable as she might think. He knew that. "Humor me," he said, "and tell me which way to go, since I have no fucking idea where we are."

The light turned green. Andy gave the truck some gas and felt Laura reach over and rest her hand on his thigh.

"Calm down," she said, then sighed and lifted her hand to point. "I'll humor you only because I love you— and take the next left."

CHAPTER
Seventeen

Laura took in the cabin. It was so familiar, but it was showing its age. For some reason, it was so much bigger in her memory than what it looked like now: smaller than an apartment, with a chimney, surrounded by rather rustic woodlands. What had to be her brother's black Lexus was parked out front.

She climbed out of the truck and closed the door. At the same time, Andy climbed out the driver' side and walked around the front, taking in everything about the place, the woods, watching as if he were trying to suss out where the danger was. Why hadn't she noticed before what he was doing? She knew he was always watching over all of them, but there didn't seem to be any movement at all here. It was quiet, eerie. She felt out of place.

"Well…" she said as she started walking.

He gestured with his chin to go as he worked a piece of gum, and she could see how he was watching her back. She strode to the door, wondering when she last had been there—when she was fourteen, she thought.

She lifted her hand to a door she'd once walked through and knocked, then listened, but she didn't hear anything.

Andy stepping over to the windows, peering in. "I don't hear anything or see anyone inside," he said as Laura knocked again. "Well, maybe he's out."

"But there's a car." Laura gestured, though she knew Andy was right. Maybe it wasn't even Chad's.

"Can I help you?" came a male voice, and she turned.

Her brother was all grown up, with short light hair, green eyes, and what looked like a week without shaving. He was wearing a tobacco-colored coat, blue jeans, and hiking boots.

"Chad…" was all she could say as she took him in. As he stared, she saw the recognition, but the smile she'd expected didn't come.

"Laura, you look the same, just a little older," he said, then took a step toward her before he dragged his gaze over to Andy and nodded. "Andy, right?"

"Yeah, it's been a long time."

She didn't look back to Andy because she could feel him standing right behind her, so close. She wondered, at what point would he step in front of her? It was his way of protecting her.

"You're likely about the last person I expected to see. Why are you here?" Chad said. Boy, did he sound cold, unwelcoming, as he stepped closer. She could feel Andy tense, and it was instinctive to reach over and touch his hand, which was right there. He must have known, as he inhaled and seemed to hesitate.

"Well, I saw the article on Mom and Dad and you and Brian," Laura said. "Congrats, by the way, on all that glory and recognition for your cause in Africa."

This time, he gave an odd laugh, an odd smile. He shook his head. "You came all the way out here because of that showpiece of Mom's? Yeah, whatever." He opened the unlocked door to the cabin and walked inside.

Laura glanced back at Andy and wasn't sure what to make of his expression, although he did gesture for her to go ahead. She stepped inside, knowing he was right behind her.

It was dark because of a lack of windows, but there was the same rickety old table and mismatched chairs, the same sofa, beige and gold and orange, which she knew was from the early seventies, someone's hand-me-downs that had come with the place.

She listened to a rattle and clank and saw Chad in the small kitchen, by the old cookstove, lifting an old coffeepot. He looked inside and then dumped in water and coffee, and he lit a match and fired the gas up. When he set the pot back down, he still hadn't said anything.

"Well, actually, Chad, I'm here about the reporters that showed up at our place this morning. They had a lot to say, a lot to ask about me, but mostly about you. Can you imagine my surprise? I tried calling the number Andy had, but it was disconnected."

He was still standing in the kitchen. This time, his back was to her, and she could see him looking out the only single-pane window in the small kitchen, his hands shoved in his back pockets. The way he stood now, she could see so much of her dad.

"So why exactly are you here, Laura? To gloat over how I'm not Mom and Dad's golden boy anymore, or to say we now have some common bond of being fallen, disgraced?"

She couldn't remember Chad ever being cruel. Andy stepped closer to her and rested his hands on her shoulders, and though she'd never tell him so, she was glad he was there.

Chad turned and faced her. He must have seen how his words stung from the way Andy was protecting her, a motion that went beyond words. He nodded and glanced to the side, distraught, emotional. She didn't know for sure. "Sorry," he said. "That was cruel. You never deserved what they did." He looked away and then flicked his gaze back to her, to Andy. His green eyes were different now, not as brilliant and bright, not filled with the kind of love and joy that filled her kids' eyes, that filled hers.

"Heard you were married," Laura said, then took in the face he made, his expression. "And the reporters also said you were gay."

This time, he gave all of his male anger to her. "Lies, all of it," he snapped.

Laura couldn't help but glance up to Andy. She didn't miss the concern, the support, the love. "Really?" she said. "Because it wouldn't matter if you are."

Chad laughed. "Well, not in Mom and Dad's eyes. You know it's a sin, and you know I'll be condemned to Hell."

The way he said it, she struggled with the ache in her chest. "That's not true, Chad. That's just Mom and Dad's twisted concept. You really believe things are that simple? They're not. Being gay isn't a sin. It's who you are."

He said nothing, and she could see the struggle.

"So you married a woman because…" Laura let it linger.

Chad took a deep, heavy breath. "Because it was expected of me. I'm a man. You find a woman, get married, get her pregnant, have kids, and spend a lifetime looking after her. It was what we were told by Dad, by Mom. There's no room for a gay man in their church, in their religion, or in the Parnell family. You should know that. So I tried to fit in and married Donna—and I do love her. She's a good woman, and now she's devastated. My daughters, too, Kaley and Maddy. The way they look at me, they see me as a monster. All because of a momentary slip, too much to drink…being caught with a man."

Andy slid his hands down, looping his arms around her, over her chest, as he pulled her against him. She could have rocked back into him, he was so comforting.

"Your kids aren't going to see you as a monster, Chad," she said. "If you're gay, you can't make yourself not be. You are what you are. Pretending to be something you're not is worse."

Chad turned on her, and she could see the anger, the fury. He must have thought better than to come any closer, though, not with Andy right there. As he gave his head a toss, she could see the inner war he seemed to be struggling with. "That's easy for you to say, Laura. Look at you. You made yourself decent and respectable now. You have a husband and a family, a place in Montana, with land, where you're part of a community and are respected."

When he said it, for a second, she had to remind herself to breathe.

"That's a lot to presume," Andy cut in, "considering you've never once reached out to us, Chad."

She felt her hand gripping his arm around her. She was so thankful for him being there now, but at the same time, she was trying to get her head around what Chad had said.

He shrugged. "I wondered for a while. Wasn't that hard to find out about you, where you are. Amazing, all the things you can find online about someone. I pieced together your life. Your children are beautiful, but they should be careful what they post up on social media for everyone to see. As a father, I feel the need to warn you."

Andy swore under his breath.

"Well, you're right about one thing," she said. "My children…" She looked back, up to Andy. "Our children are the best, and we love them. At the same time, Chad, we support our kids with who they are, with what they want to be. They're not perfect, and we're not perfect, and we don't expect them to follow in our footsteps. We want them to make their own mistakes, to make their own choices, because we can't live their lives for them. Nor can we expect them to do what we want them to. You're a gay man living the life of a heterosexual. Like, how twisted and fucked up is that? Maybe ask yourself, Chad, whose life you're living."

"You wouldn't get it, Laura," Chad snapped and leaned toward her. He didn't seem to care that Andy was there now, and she took in a brother she didn't know.

"I get a lot more than you think," she said, but he shook his head.

"You were gone. You were never spoken of, Laura. That's how big a disappointment you were and still are."

Boy, he could be cruel. At any other time, she'd likely have been reeling from the hurt.

"Watch yourself," Andy said, but Chad didn't seem to pay him any mind, too wrapped up in his anger.

"Well, I'm sorry for them," Laura said. "If what happened to me happened to one of our kids, Andy and I would never have disgraced or treated her so badly. I guess the difference between Mom and Dad and me and Andy is that we really love our kids, and we accept them for who they are, not who we expect them to be."

Chad said nothing, appearing hard and unforgiving. For a minute, she thought it was her he was angry at, but she realized it was self-loathing. Had he always been like this? "What do you want from me, Laura?" he said, crossing his arms.

She felt Andy's hands on her arms now, sliding down, supporting her, holding her. "Well, nothing, Chad, to be honest. I have a life, a great life, one I never expected to have, but when a reporter comes knocking on my door, asking the kind of questions they are…"

"I got it." He cut her off so abruptly. "Just tell them it's not true. That's all you need to say."

"My wife isn't going to lie, Chad, and neither am I," Andy said. "Maybe you should think who you're really lying to. It's not just your wife. You're not being fair to your kids or yourself by pretending to be someone you're not. The question is already there, so what if you're gay? Just be it. Be happy."

The look Chad gave him was pure horror. "If I chose that life, then I wouldn't have a life. I would be disowned by my mom and dad, and I've built my life around the church, their church. I'm part of the mission. I would have to give all that up, and I won't do that. Maybe you think it's that easy and simple, but it's not. I would lose everything I have, my reputation, my home, my family. There isn't a choice, not for me and not for Brian, either, but then, what does he care? He's happy with his life, his wife, his kids, the perfect everything. He told me to get my head together, and I got my mom's marching orders, too.

"They told me to pack a bag, go to the cabin, and get my priorities in line and my thinking clear about who I am and who I'm supposed to be. I have responsibilities, a wife and daughters and a life that doesn't allow such a choice. They say I'm confused and time away is all I need to get clear. She's handling things for me, or so it seemed, but apparently not enough. She wouldn't be happy with the reporters calling on you. Then there's Dad, with his look of disapproval." He inclined his head, and Laura just stared at him, understanding. Being gay would never have been okay with them. They never had believed it was anything other than a state of mind.

"Do you really listen to yourself and what you're saying?" she said. "Who cares what she thinks, Chad?"

"I care!" he shouted. "Don't you fucking get it? She's my mother, my family. I mean, what are you, who are you? You're just a girl who got pregnant and made a better life. You just don't get it, Laura. It's not as black and white as you think. This is a family, and when you're part of a family, you don't get to be selfish. You have to give things up, and there are tough choices to be made. You can't be who you want to be, Laura, not when you have family depending on you." He flicked his gaze over to her, and she wasn't sure what he was thinking—disgust, anger, what?

"Times have changed, Chad," she said. "We don't live in a time anymore where girls are sent away when they get pregnant, and all anyone knows is that they're with relatives. You're not ostracized for being gay anymore, either. Even many of the churches are now recognizing that homosexuality isn't a lifestyle choice. In fact, they're even recognizing marriage between two women, two men. It's not condemned in many of the—"

"It is in ours, Laura, and Mom and Dad would drop dead first before ever admitting that they were wrong, that the church is wrong, that everything they ever believed couldn't be right." The way he spoke, it sounded as if he was trying to convince himself.

"I don't know what else to say to you, Chad, except I'm sorry for you," Laura said.

He just shook his head and looked away. She wasn't sure what he was looking at, but then he turned off the stove as the pot boiled. "I used to think you owed me," he said. "I thought about you and your life, your happiness. Seeing those pictures of you and your family, the ones your kids posted, it didn't seem fair to see you so happy."

Just hearing those words stunned her. Why would he ever believe she owed him anything?

"So it was you who sent the letter," she said.

He didn't look at her, just stared down at the pot on the stove, and she heard Andy swear under his breath, felt him step back and drag his hand over his chin with a scrape of whiskers.

Chad flicked his gaze over to her, resting his hands

on the sides of the stove. "I was drunk," he said. "I'm sorry."

She didn't know what to say. "Why? What do you think I owe you?" She didn't have to turn around to know that Andy was right there.

"Nothing—everything," he said. This time, he lifted his gaze. "I was angry, am angry, that you're so happy. Like, how fair is that?"

Andy stepped around her, beside her. His hand was there, and it was so easy to just slip hers into his.

"So you hate me because I'm happy?" she said. "That's pretty messed up, Chad."

He looked so sad as he looked at her, then dragged his gaze over to Andy. "You're right, it is," he said and shook his head. "I guess you are the lucky one after all, Laura."

For a minute, she didn't know how to respond, as he just stared at her, his expression numb, unfeeling. "How so?" she finally said.

He just looked at her as if she didn't get it before he said, "Because you got out."

What was it about watching her sleep?

Instead of being selfish and waking her to satisfy his incessant need, he just watched her. He swore with Laura, his appetite for sex was insatiable. There was just something about touching her, lying beside her, loving her, that he couldn't get enough of. She was gorgeous and beautiful and his, and there were times he just wanted to hold her.

Then there were times her need outmatched his. The night before, she'd pulled him from a light sleep, straddling him and slipping around him, riding him. He'd pressed his head back into the pillow and held her as she moved. It was mind-blowing, and at times he couldn't stop from shouting out at the way she kissed him, touched him.

Yet here she was, sound asleep now, and for the first time, he swore it was as if a weight had been lifted from her. Even though there had been such peace in their life throughout the years they were together, there was something comforting about closing those doors and knowing nothing else could be lurking in the wings to take them down.

He heard her stir, and she turned, blinking and yawning, her hand touching him, his chest, his shoulder, as he leaned over her.

"How long've you been awake?" she asked.

They were in the double bed of a motel halfway between Sandpoint and home. Seeing how tired she was, he'd pulled in there instead of driving home in the dark.

"A while," he said. "Just watching you sleep."

Her eyes flickered with mischief as she reached under the sheets and touched him.

"Hey, hey!" he said. "Be careful there, or we could be late checking out and getting back on the road."

She was smiling, teasing. "And maybe I wouldn't mind. It's just time. We have lots of that."

He ran his fingers over her cheek, her hair, as she kissed his neck and shoulder. "Hmm," was all he said. "And what about your parents? We've come this far. Anyone else you want to see, talk to?"

He still remembered how Chad had shook his hand and said nothing else to Laura before she started out the door without a glance back. It was him who had been left alone with her brother.

"Don't contact my wife again," Andy had said, and Chad had said nothing, standing alone and miserable.

"Nope," Laura replied and shook her head. "We came here, and that's enough. Don't let this go to your head—well, I know it will anyway, but I'm glad you came with me." She rolled her eyes, likely because of how arrogant he could be.

He just grunted. "So next time you won't argue with me, because I'm always right."

She burst out laughing, then wrapped her arms around his neck. "So how about showing me just how late we can get back on the road?"

Yeah, he really loved her. He leaned in and pressed a kiss to her lips, intent on showing her exactly what she meant to him.

"I love you, Andy Friessen," she whispered in his ear when he broke the kiss, and he really looked at her, seeing the love she couldn't hide from him.

"I love you more, Laura Friessen."

Turn the page for a sneak peek of
ALL ABOUT DEVON
Available in print, eBook & audio

All About Devon

New York Times & *USA Today* bestselling author Lorhainne Eckhart brings young love and redemption in this Friessen family novella about a sweet small town romance.

Devon Reed has his girlfriend's father to thank for getting him back in school—but he knows Andy Friessen is like a pit bull where Sara is concerned, so he needs to keep his best foot forward with this man. In fact, Devon still can't believe he's been accepted into the Friessen family.

Despite their differences, Devon struggles to admit that he wants to keep Sara in his life because he really loves her. When he receives an unexpected invite to visit his mother, who's serving time in prison, it's Sara who insists that maybe, just maybe, his mother has changed.

He decides to give his mother a chance, but does that

mean pushing Sara, the best thing that has ever happened to him, away?

All About Devon

Devon stared at the house, tapping his fingers on the steering wheel of his old Mazda. Dirty and dusty, with a red flashing oil light that would never go out, the car was in much need of some detailing—as if that would ever happen, considering he'd just poured his last twenty dollars into the tank so he could drive all the way out to here and yonder to see his girl. With her pit bull of a father at the door, he still couldn't figure out how he had ever been invited in.

The screen door of the house opened, and there was Sara: beautiful—no, gorgeous and blond, and wow, that smile. She was definitely not the stereotypical blond airhead. She lifted her hand in a wave from the porch, and Devon yanked open his door and stepped out.

Holy shit, there was her dad. He had to fight the urge to freeze as he took in Andy Friessen, all six solid feet of him, with no smile, perpetually pissed off, standing behind his daughter with his hand on her shoulder, staring him down. He closed the door and walked around the front of the car, not missing the way Andy's eyes tracked his every move.

"Everything okay? Was wondering if you were going to get out of the car," Sara called out.

Maybe she was messing with him. Did she have any idea what it was like to be on the other side of her dad? The way he watched Devon, that one look alone said there was absolutely nothing he could hide from him, and if he made one wrong move with his daughter, he'd put him in the ground.

"Yeah, just…"

The truth was that he'd been getting up his nerve to face the questions that always came from Andy Friessen: How was school, his grades, his job? Was he keeping his nose clean or fucking up with the wrong choices? Then there was Sara and all the do-over dates they'd had over the past few months. But she was worth it, which was likely why he was walking into the lion's den yet again.

Sara must have known, as she glanced back over her shoulder, where Andy still lingered, arms now crossed over his chest. "Dad came out to say hi," she said, and he didn't miss how she rolled her eyes, her tone dripping with sarcasm.

As he stood at the bottom of the steps, Sara glanced back up to her dad again, and just that one look alone had Andy's gaze softening. The man would do anything for his kids, and Devon knew that, understood that. In fact, it made him question what this was with Sara, this attraction, this interest, despite the two sides of the tracks they were on.

"Heard you're top of your class," Andy said.

Devon paused, staring up at the man who'd paid for his school that year. "And you heard that from…?" He knew there was an edge to his tone, as he wondered whether paying his way meant Andy Friessen was also getting continual updates from his professors.

"From Sara," Andy said. "She brags about you, how smart you are, how easy you find your classes."

Right, from Sara. He dropped his gaze and took in the girl who had stolen his heart. Her mysterious green eyes were at times filled with mischief and the kind of sass he still wasn't ready to admit he loved.

"Don't be so modest, Devon," Sara said. "Dad's not spying on you, although I wouldn't put it past him, considering I'm pretty sure he has all my teachers on speed dial and checks in with them regularly to find out what I'm doing, thinking, and…"

"And whether you're actually participating in class and doing the work or just wasting time," Andy jumped in.

For a second, as Devon watched Andy, he thought maybe he was serious. Then his gaze softened, and the same sharp teasing he often saw in Sara appeared there. So that was who she got it from. When his gaze lifted to Devon, though, everything turned serious again. Yup, he needed to watch his step.

"You didn't elaborate on school," Andy said. "Come on, Devon. Grades, classes, prospects?" He actually gestured to prompt him.

"Grades are good—it comes easy. Done next week for the summer, but no offers," Devon replied. He was the only one without an internship, but then again, he was the only one with his kind of background.

"Unusual, isn't that?" Andy said. "Understood you should have any number of firms making some type of offer for the summer."

He just stared at Andy, wondering why he didn't get it. "You know what my classmates have in common?" he said. His hands were shoved in his gray hoodie pocket as he stared up at Andy, not missing the way Sara was staring up at him too. He thought about the names the professor had posted on the board with an offer of jobs for the summer. They were burned into his memory.

Andy had a way of silently watching people that could make anyone uncomfortable. He just waited, so Devon shrugged, and Andy finally pulled in a breath. "I wouldn't have a clue, Devon, so enlighten me."

"Not one of them is from the wrong side of the tracks," Devon said. "Each has parents with some kind of pull in town. Todd's father is a lawyer and his mom is a specialist at the hospital, Matt's parents own that computer shop with chains across the state, Linda's dad is a contractor, John's parents are both financial specialists, Lydia's parents are divorced but have the kind of jobs where tuition is just pocket change, Ryder's parents are real estate moguls, and Sid lives with his grandparents, his grandfather being the dean of the university."

Yeah, he didn't miss their shocked expressions. Sara glanced again to her dad, who was staring at Devon with an odd expression.

"So you're saying that privilege is involved here?" Andy said, his arms pulled over his chest.

Devon blinked and inhaled, feeling himself on a slippery slope. "Well, of course. It always is." He had to roll his shoulders.

"And maybe the color of their skin?" Andy didn't move. He stood so tall, and Devon could feel the strength ooze from him. It was in his voice, the way he talked and stared down at him, giving him the feeling he could crush him if he chose to.

"At times it is, yes—but Linda is Hispanic…" And Sid was as black as he was. Devon pictured their faces. He couldn't relate to one of them.

"So this isn't about race then," Andy said, and Devon could feel himself under a microscope.

"In a way, but no," he said. What was it, then? He still couldn't relate to one of their lives, what they had or what they did.

"So let me ask you this, Devon." Andy gestured to him before crossing his arms over his chest again. Sara lifted a brow, and Devon wondered what that meant. He was exceptional at reading people, situations, yet here he was in a scenario he'd never expected to be in. "Could it be that those kids—and, by the way, good recall to be able to ramble off a list of names and their parental connections—but could it not be that the kids who were offered an internship are just better qualified?"

He knew he made a face. "What? No. Are you kidding? There's no way. As you stated, I'm top of the class, with the highest marks, yet here they are, a bunch of brown-nosing, privileged…" He stopped talking at the way Andy and Sara both looked at him as if they were humoring him.

"Or hard workers without a chip on their shoulders?" Andy cut in. Even Sara's gaze softened a bit.

"I don't have a chip on my shoulder, and my grades speak for themselves," Devon said. "I should have been top pick instead, but I was never approached by my professor, never had an offer. It should have been me, so how else should I look at it?"

"Grades are important, but what's even more so is

personality, being a team player. Those qualities are often the coveted icing on the cake. Ask yourself, Devon, are you a team player, or are you the lone wolf with an attitude? You're smart, brilliant, but sometimes, especially in an internship, getting your foot in the door of a company, you need to be a team player, the kind of person who gets along and works well with others. I bet if you take a step back and look at every one of those kids who were offered an internship and the companies that offered them, you'll see those kids are the ones who showed your professor that they can work together, get along, and be an asset to a company, kind of like good yes-men. Although the lone wolf is a coveted asset, it isn't for a company looking to bring in summer interns to do their bidding. They want youth who are willing to work together and not create ripples, disputes, and division in a company. So think about that."

Boy, he'd never had someone put him in his place quite like that before. He thought about his classmates, popular, partyers—and, yup, always joking and laughing with the professor.

"That's not me," Devon said. "You expect me to change who I am and fit into a mold to get a job?"

This time he was positive, by the twitch at the edge of Andy's mouth, that he was doing his best not to laugh at him. He shook his head. "Nope, not what I'm saying. You are who you are, but just don't go putting a label on everyone else to find an excuse whenever you're not picked. Let me ask you something: The jobs they were picked for and the companies that offered them, just how comfortable would you be doing that kind of work?"

For a second, he just stared as he considered,

picturing himself as a mindless yes-man working for some useless, uptight corporate CEO.

"Right, just as I thought," Andy said. "You're top of your class, so figure out what you want to do, who you want to work for, and go after that. Don't wait around for something to come to you. You go after something. That's how you get somewhere, and that's what separates you from everyone else." He gestured to Devon, who again fisted his hands in his hoodie pocket, before resting his hand on Sara's shoulder and glancing down at her. "So you said dinner and a movie, or are you staying here tonight?"

Devon realized he wasn't being addressed.

"Movie, right?" Sara said, glancing over to him, and all he could feel was the empty wallet in his back pocket.

"Lorhainne Eckhart is one of my go to authors when I want a guaranteed good book. So many twists and turns, but also so much love and such a strong sense of family."

(LORA W., REVIEWER)

New York Times & USA Today bestseller Lorhainne Eckhart is best known for writing Raw Relatable Real Romance where "Morals and family are running themes." As one fan calls her, she is the "Queen of the family saga." (aherman) writing "the ups and downs of what goes on within a family but also with some suspense, angst and of course a bit of romance thrown in for good measure." Follow Lorhainne on Bookbub to receive alerts on New Releases and Sales and join her mailing list at LorhainneEckhart.com for her Monday Blog, all book news, giveaways and FREE reads. With over 120 books, audiobooks, and multiple series published and available at all, retailers now translated into six languages. She is a multiple recipient of the Readers' Favorite Award for Suspense and Romance, and lives in the Pacific Northwest on an island, is the mother of three, her oldest has autism and she is an advocate for never giving up on your dreams.

"Lorhainne Eckhart has this uncanny way of just hitting the spot every time with her books."

(CAROLINE L., REVIEWER)

The O'Connells: *The O'Connells of Livingston, Montana are not your typical family. A riveting collection of stories surrounding the ups and downs of what goes on within a family but also with some suspense, angst and of course a bit of romance thrown in for good measure. "I thought I loved the Friessens, but I absolutely adore the O'Connell's. Each and every book has different genres of stories, but the one thing in common is how she is able to wrap it around the family, which is the heart of each story." (C. Logue)*

The Friessens: *An emotional big family*

romance series, the Friessen family siblings find their relationships tested, lay their hearts on the line, and discover lasting love! "Lorhainne Eckhart is one of my go to authors when I want a guaranteed good book. So many twists and turns, but also so much love and such a strong sense of family." (Lora W., Reviewer)

The Parker Sisters: *The Parker Sisters are a close-knit family, and like any other family they have their ups and downs. Eckhart has crafted another intense family drama… "The character development is outstanding, and the emotional investment is high…" (Aherman, Reviewer)*

The McCabe Brothers: *Join the five McCabe siblings on their journeys to the dark and dangerous side of love! An intense, exhilarating collection of romantic thrillers you won't want to miss. — "Eckhart has a new series that is definitely worth the read. The queen of the family saga started this series with a spin-off of her wildly successful Friessen series." From a Readers' Favorite award—winning author and "queen of the family saga" (Aherman)*

Billy Jo McCabe Mystery: *The social worker and the cop, an unlikely couple drawn together on a small, secluded Pacific Northwest island where nothing is as it*

In the Silence
In the Charm
Unexpected Consequences
It Was Always You
The First Time I Saw You
Welcome to My Arms
Welcome to Boston
I'll Always Love You
Ground Rules
A Reason to Breathe
You Are My Everything
Anything For You
The Homecoming
Stay Away From My Daughter
The Bad Boy
A Place of Our Own
The Visitor
All About Devon
Long Past Dawn
How to Heal a Heart
Keep Me In Your Heart

The O'Connells
The Neighbor
The Third Call
The Secret Husband
The Quiet Day
The Commitment
The Missing Father
The Hometown Hero
Justice
The Family Secret
The Fallen O'Connell

The Return of the O'Connells
And The She Was Gone
The Stalker
The O'Connell Family Christmas
The Girl Next Door
Broken Promises
The Gatekeeper
The Hunted

The McCabe Brothers
Don't Stop Me (Vic)
Don't Catch Me (Chase)
Don't Run From Me (Aaron)
Don't Hide From Me (Luc)
Don't Leave Me (Claudia)
Out of Time

A Billy Jo McCabe Mystery
Nothing As it Seems
Hiding in Plain Sight
The Cold Case
The Trap
Above the Law
The Stranger at the Door
The Children
The Last Stand
The Charity
The Sacrifice

The Street Fighter
Finding Home
Finding Honor

The Wilde Brothers
The One (Joe and Margaret)
The Honeymoon, A Wilde Brothers Short
Friendly Fire (Logan and Julia)
Not Quite Married, A Wilde Brothers Short
A Matter of Trust (Ben and Carrie)
The Reckoning, A Wilde Brothers Christmas
Traded (Jake)
Unforgiven (Samuel)
The Holiday Bride

Married in Montana
His Promise
Love's Promise
A Promise of Forever

The Parker Sisters
Thrill of the Chase
The Dating Game
Play Hard to Get
What We Can't Have
Go Your Own Way
A June Wedding

Kate & Walker
One Night
Edge of Night
Last Night

Walk the Right Road Series
The Choice
Lost and Found
Merkaba

Bounty
Blown Away: The Final Chapter
He Came Back

The Saved Series
Saved
Vanished
Captured

Single Titles
Loving Christine

9 781998 775705